DALE

Quarry in the Quince

Lovely Lethal Gardens 17

QUARRY IN THE QUINCE: LOVELY LETHAL GARDENS,
BOOK 17
Dale Mayer
Valley Publishing

ISBN-13: 978-1-773365-87-9
Print Edition

Books in This Series

About This Book

A new cozy mystery series from *USA Today* best-selling author Dale Mayer. Follow gardener and amateur sleuth Doreen Montgomery—and her amusing and mostly lovable cat, dog, and parrot—as they catch murderers and solve crimes in lovely Kelowna, British Columbia.

Riches to rags ... Chaos is down ... Everyone loves sparkly rings ... Some more than others!
Who knew a simple trip to the consignment store would find Wendy being strong-armed by two strangers? *So* not allowed—especially as it could affect Doreen getting her month-end check! Trying to get to the bottom of this is one convoluted story to sort out. It involves Bernard—an eccentric and handsome older man, who had a very young fiancée in his life—the breakup, and the resulting theft.

Corporal Mack Moreau is not at all happy with Doreen's new male friend, Bernard, who has the money to keep her in the style she was accustomed to. However, Mack is happy Doreen is staying out of his cases, if only she could stay out of trouble! Then again, Doreen can find trouble like this without any effort on her part. At least this time she also befriends another Kelowna icon, who lives behind Wendy's store and who is well-known for her quince jams and jellies.

Yet a big shiny reward from Bernard awaits someone who solves the theft and how it involves Wendy and the jam icon. Maybe—just maybe—that someone could be Doreen.

Sign up to be notified of all Dale's releases here!
http://smarturl.it/dmnewsletter

Chapter 1

Saturday, Second Week of August

MACK MOREAU REACHED out several times to Doreen Montgomery to update her, to check up on her, then to take her—and her animals—over to his mom's for mid-morning tea. Millicent even had special treats for Doreen's pets. Afterward, Goliath remained perfectly content to lie at their feet on the porch. Of course Thaddeus sat on Doreen's shoulder, yet was oddly quiet during this visit. Doreen let Mugs off his leash, knowing he wouldn't go farther than just sniffing all around Millicent's yard.

Doreen hopped up, wandered around the garden with him, and made a mental list of things to fix.

As she returned to them, Doreen looked over at his mother. "I'll come by tomorrow and take care of those weeds," she promised, fully aware that the ones right in front of the older woman's view bothered her terribly.

Millicent smiled gratefully. "Thank you. I know you've been busy with other things. Still, it does feel like I'm wasting your time, but I'd appreciate it, if you could come by."

Doreen laughed. "You're saving me." She glanced at

Mack. "I keep getting into trouble, when I'm not working."

Millicent shook her head. "What you do is very important, and it helps my son."

"Well, I try," Doreen replied quietly, "but I work in a much different way."

At that, the older woman nodded in full understanding. "You two make a good pair."

Doreen flushed and refused to look at Mack. "Well, we certainly make a pair," she finally muttered. "One who gets into trouble and one who tries to keep the other out of trouble."

At that, Mack laughed. "Isn't that the truth? Even when you're supposedly out of trouble, you're in trouble."

"And yet I don't try to be," she stated, looking over at him. "But sometimes people tell me things, and I guess my brain works in a weird way."

"A weird and wonderful way," Millicent noted firmly. Then she chuckled. "And I'm really glad. It's shaken up Mack's life, and that's good. He was getting a little too set in his ways."

He stared at his mother in surprise.

She shrugged. "You and your brother both." She leaned forward and whispered, "Did you hear that Nick's looking at coming back to town?"

At that, Mack smiled and nodded. "That would be nice, wouldn't it?"

"It'd be really nice." Millicent looked at the gardens and sighed. "I sure hope he can make it happen soon."

Doreen turned to her, frowning. "Did he give you a time frame?"

"No, he didn't. He did say that he'd make another trip here. He has to see somebody who's been avoiding him."

Mack raised an eyebrow and turned slowly to glare at Doreen.

She flushed and slunk lower in her chair. "I wonder who that could be?" she asked in an innocent tone.

Mack sighed heavily. "Does he need to talk to you?"

"I don't know," she replied. "There has been a phone message or two, but, over the last couple days, honestly, I just haven't wanted to talk to anybody."

He nodded. "And I get that, but you know if he needs you …"

She sniffed. "I don't want to deal with that."

He burst out laughing. "Yet you contacted Nick. And you know what he does for a living."

She winced.

"And he is doing this for free."

She sighed. "Fine," she agreed. "If he doesn't come soon, I'll give him a call."

"I'm hoping he'll come this weekend," Millicent said, "but I can't count on that. He is a busy man." She looked at Mack, at Doreen, and then again at Mack, back to Doreen. "Is Nick helping you out with something, dear?"

"Ever since my lovely lawyer died and left my divorce in a mess, your son Nick's been helping me clear it up."

"Oh, that's lovely." She beamed. "He's such a good boy. He's always willing to help."

At that, even Mack rolled his eyes. "Now, if you're coming back here tomorrow to work in Mom's garden, and you already have a worklist of what you need to do here, can we head to the beach today?" he asked Doreen.

"Sure." She bounced to her feet. "You didn't mention that lately."

"Nope, I didn't," he noted. "I figured, if I mentioned

3

paddleboards, you'd run screaming in the opposite direction."

She turned and glared at him. "Please tell me that we're not trying that again." He just raised an eyebrow, and she sighed. "Fine. As long as we'll head to the beach today, I wanted to stop and talk to Wendy today too."

He frowned. "On a Saturday?"

She nodded. "You're right. It's probably a busy day for her, isn't it?"

"If it's money you're after, why don't you wait until Monday morning?"

"Fine. Let's go to the beach, get soaking wet, and … have some food." She looked at him hopefully.

He nodded. "I have a picnic packed."

She beamed. "Why didn't you say so?" she cried out. She leaned over, gave the older woman a hug, and said, "I'll see you tomorrow."

"Good enough." Millicent smiled. "You young people go have a nice day."

And, with that, the two of them, along with the three pets, headed out. Settled in Mack's truck, Doreen said, "I still worry about Wendy." She felt more than saw Mack glance in her direction.

"Has she contacted you since?"

"No."

"If she's not ready to talk, … there's nothing you or I can do. It might be nothing at all to worry about."

"Yes, it felt … off. Wrong somehow." She pondered the little she'd seen and Wendy's disturbing reaction.

Mack pointed. "Behind Wendy's shop are Esther's famous quince trees." He took his eyes off the road for a moment. "Esther makes the best quince jam and sold it for years at the Kelowna market. I have to tell you, her jam was 'the' product everyone bought back then. Even now, the market still is a lively place, but her jam? … That's the jam." And he burst out laughing at his joke.

"Quince?" Immediately an image of the fragrant pear-looking fruit popped into her head. "I thought they didn't taste great."

"They need to be cooked first, I believe. Honestly, I've never tried to handle them myself. The only quince I've ever eaten was Esther's jam. I've bought dozens of jars over the years. And those suckers trade like hot commodities." He shook his head at that. "I wish I could get her recipe, but she was crotchety back in the day. I can't imagine how she is now." He turned a corner and drove toward the beach. "Her place backs onto the alley at the rear of Wendy's shop."

Doreen looked at him in surprise, then giggled.

He shot a glance at her, a big smile on his face. "What's so funny?"

"We just finished *Poison in the Pansies*," she said, her laughter rolling out louder and louder. "Now we have *quince* in the picture. And *Q* follows *P* in the alphabet. So what kind of case works with the letter *Q*?" In between giggles, and Mugs woofing, and now Thaddeus cawing at the noise, she finally got out, "*Quarry*. That works. *Quarry in the Quince.*"

And she went off in gales of laughter.

Indeed, it was a glorious day.

Chapter 2

Monday Morning

S ATURDAY HAD BEEN a lovely day. The next day had also been nice, as Doreen finished up some gardening at Millicent's place and then spent the rest of the day at home with her animals. Mack had been called into work, so knowing she had the day to herself, she grabbed a book, sat down at the river, and just enjoyed being alone and having fun. She checked in with Nan a couple times to make sure she was doing okay, and, outside of making several cups of tea and some toast or peanut butter sandwiches, she spent the rest of the weekend just relaxing.

When Monday morning dawned bright and clear, she got up and got dressed, put on the coffee, opened up the back door to let out the animals, and then sat on the patio with her coffee, checking the time.

As soon as it was ten to eight, she looked down at Mugs and asked, "What do you think? Is Wendy open yet?"

He woofed beside her and rolled over to give her a belly to rub. She looked around at Thaddeus, who was wandering up and down the deck railing, marching in some weird step but seemingly quite content. Goliath, completely immune to the antics of the others, was asleep atop the outdoor table, with his paws sky-high. She reached over and petted him too, startling him awake so that he immediately rolled over and jumped to his feet and stared at her with a hard look.

She winced. "Sorry, buddy. I wasn't trying to wake you up."

He gave a *meow* and threw himself down onto his side again, letting his head drop with a heavy *clunk*.

"Hey, hey, hey," she said. "Apparently you're still tired." She reached out and gently rubbed his belly, but that meant she had to remove her hand from Mugs's belly. When her hand returned to pet him, Mugs immediately woofed and kicked his legs in the air, as if trying to roll over. She smirked at his antics, bent down again, and petted his belly.

"We'll have a piece of toast," she told them. "And then we'll see if we can get some grocery money off Wendy." And, with that, she got up, tossed back the last of her first cup of coffee, returned to the kitchen, put on a piece of toast, and poured a second cup.

As she stood here, staring out at her backyard and the beautiful morning, she wondered at Wendy's actions the last couple of times Doreen had seen her. She hoped today Wendy was back to normal, but obviously something was going on. Hearing Mack's words repeat in her mind, Doreen wondered if Wendy would talk to Doreen about it. She decided to walk, even though it would take a lot longer, but she figured that Wendy probably wouldn't have her check ready until at least nine o'clock.

With the animals in tow, she headed to the consignment store. It did take a bit to get there, particularly with Mugs stopping to sniff every bush and Goliath seemingly plopping down to rest at every tenth sidewalk block. Thaddeus was content to pace up and down on her shoulder, bob his head, and sing a song. She laughed at his antics because it was a well-known part of his personality that she thoroughly enjoyed.

By the time she and her crew got to the block where Wendy's store was, Doreen headed around the back and came up the alleyway. No sign of the big white van, which was good. The alley was more for delivery trucks to service the businesses on one side. On the other side were residences, all backed with fences, so the owners didn't look out on the alleyway and any off-loading going on here.

Doreen walked up and knocked on the rear door to Wendy's shop. When she got no answer, she knocked again. When she still got no answer, she tried the doorknob, but it was locked. Frowning, she walked with the animals around to the front and pulled open the front door. It did open, but the lights inside were off. She called out, "Hello? Wendy, are you here?"

She looked down at the animals and realized that's why she shouldn't have brought them. Having animals around always added an element of chaos, which was normal with pets and children too, but, going into a store like this, the animals could be more of a problem.

All of a sudden the lights turned on, and Wendy bustled forward, a big smile plastered on her face. "Good morning," she sang out.

Doreen looked at her in surprise and explained, "I tried the back door, but you didn't answer."

She shrugged. "I was probably in the washroom." She looked down at the animals. "You know, if the store were busy, I wouldn't let them in."

"I know," Doreen muttered. "I wanted to walk and to

get a bit of exercise, so it didn't occur to me to think about the end result of bringing them inside with me."

Wendy laughed. "Well, it's early, and I'm not likely to have anybody immediately anyway." She motioned at Doreen. "So come on in. If we do get customers wanting to shop and to look around, I may ask you to step outside with your animals."

"That's fine. I just wondered ..." And then she hesitated. "I wondered if you had any money for me."

"Ah." She nodded. "I did mention that, didn't I?"

"Yes," Doreen agreed.

"More fool me." She shrugged and pointed to the back. "Let me go take a look." And, with that, she disappeared into her little office.

Doreen wandered the store, looking at some of the clothes. Some of it was beautiful stuff. The last thing she wanted to do was spend her money here. Still, she reached out and touched one of the pieces; it had been a long time since Doreen had had something new. A holdover from her previous life apparently, but she still wanted that joy of something new. She shook her head. "You'll have time for that later," she muttered. "Stand strong now."

Just then Wendy walked back out again. "Did you say something?"

"I was talking to myself, reminding me that I don't have money to spend right now, but I will later," she shared cheerfully.

Wendy laughed. "Money's like that," she agreed.

Yet an overly happy tone filled her voice that made Doreen stare at her quizzically. "Are you feeling okay?" she asked.

At that, Wendy grimaced. "And here I figured everybody

would think I was having a great day."

"Maybe don't try so hard," Doreen suggested in a quiet voice.

Almost immediately the overly positive look dropped from Wendy's face. Instead she stared at Doreen with a haunted look. "Let's just say the last few weeks have been challenging," she muttered.

Doreen looked around at the very fully stocked store. "Is business that bad?"

"It's that kind of a business," she noted. "Lots of cycles. Lots of ups and downs, lots of good days and bad days," she muttered. "Yet overall it's okay." And then she laughed and held out a check. "And, in your case, hopefully today's a good day."

Doreen looked down at the check, and it was over $600.00. She beamed. "Thank you." Then Doreen turned and looked down at her animals in joy. "We get to eat for the month."

Mugs immediately barked and wrapped himself around her legs. Goliath, who was lying inside the front door, completely ignored Doreen, except for his tail twitching, making heavy *thunk, thunk* noises on the hardwood floor.

"Is that really all the money you have?" Wendy asked curiously.

At that, Doreen shrugged. "I make a little bit doing gardening and stuff. However, ... I do have money coming—sometime, eventually. Meanwhile, it's just tight right now."

"Yeah, I hear you on the tight part," Wendy muttered. "Sometimes when we say things are tight, we don't realize just how tight it can be, for ourselves and others."

As Doreen nodded, a heavy banging came at Wendy's back door. She caught the look on Wendy's face and noted all the color had sagged from it. "You want me to answer that?" Doreen offered immediately.

"No," Wendy replied immediately. "I don't want either of us to answer it."

At that, Doreen faced her. "Okay, you need to tell me what's going on."

Wendy shook her head. "No, I can't do that. And, besides, it's bad enough that I'm in trouble. I don't want you in trouble too."

"Maybe you should explain to me what kind of trouble we're talking about. Maybe I can help you."

Wendy shook her head again.

Doreen sighed. "Remember? Remember all the stuff I've been doing since I arrived in town?"

Wendy stopped and frowned. "It's dangerous," she replied. "And I don't even know how dangerous."

"Another reason to let me get involved," Doreen added. "Maybe we can defuse this before it gets any uglier."

"I don't think so," she argued. "They're looking for something. Something they say was dropped off by accident, and they think I have it."

At that, Doreen stared at her in surprise. "How do you drop something off by accident?"

"Yeah, that's the problem. Somebody assumed that I was operating more like a pawnshop, came in here, and asked if I could buy something off her for cash right now. I didn't like anything about the scenario, and I told her no. She left, but apparently the item didn't go with her," she explained. "I don't know what happened to it."

"And you've told these people?"

"I have, but they don't believe me, and it was a piece supposedly worth a lot of money."

"So why you, and why not like a jewelry store?"

"I don't know. I think because she thought I could give her cash."

"So she was in trouble?"

At that, Wendy slowly nodded.

"*Great,*" Doreen murmured. "Do you have any idea who it was? Was it somebody you know?"

"The woman?" Wendy asked and then shook her head. "No, I've never seen her before. I figured that maybe she was just in town visiting and took an opportunity to make some quick money."

"And do you think the item was stolen?"

She winced. "I don't know that. I guess I worry that that is a possibility. She didn't say it was stolen. Those guys bothering me didn't say it was stolen. I don't … I just don't know." She shook her head. "But now these guys seem to think that I have it, and they keep threatening me."

"And you haven't contacted the police, have you?"

Wendy shook her head again. "No," she replied in a small voice.

"And you know that'll just make the local authorities angry too."

"I know. I know it'll make the police angry. It'll make these guys angry," she added. "I just don't know what to do anymore. I was hoping these guys would go away and leave me alone."

"Why would they?" she asked. "If for no other reason, they probably think that you're a big score for them some-how now."

"Why? I run a secondhand store." Wendy threw her arms wide to encompass the merchandise on the hangers behind her. "I'm hardly making more than a living here."

"That's a good point too," Doreen noted thoughtfully.

Once again the doorknob on the rear exit rattled, with whomever trying to get in.

Making a determined move toward it, Doreen said, "Let me talk to them. I at least want to see their faces."

"What good will that do?" Wendy cried out, trailing slowly behind Doreen.

"Do you have them on camera?"

"They broke it," she replied. "Almost the first day that they were here, they snapped it. And no, I haven't done anything about it."

"Of course. And you don't have the money to fix it, do you?"

At that, Wendy shook her head.

Doreen nodded thoughtfully. "Don't let these guys see you." She walked with Mugs to the back, opening the door just when it started rattling again, surprising the men. She braced herself to have somebody jump forward and push their way inside, only to have the two men stop and stare at her. "May I help you?" she asked. "Wendy's not in today. I'm here to look after the store."

Immediately one man frowned.

She frowned right back, giving him a hard look. "And why aren't you using the front door?" she asked. "Everybody knows that the back isn't for customers."

"I'm not a customer," he snarled.

She studied him, one eyebrow raised. She looked him up and down and frowned. "So I'm not sure what you're here for then. Are you looking to buy your wife a present?"

He flushed. "Get out of my way," he demanded. As he went to shove her away, Mugs growled deep and long.

He backed up, looked down at the dog, and asked,

"Why is a dog here?"

"Well, since her security system isn't working anymore—and I'm not exactly sure what happened there—I decided to bring my dog into work to help keep out the riffraff."

He stiffened at that. "Did you just call me riffraff?"

"I'm not sure what to call you," she noted curiously. "What is your name?"

He stared at her, backed up, and replied, "It doesn't matter what my name is. Tell Wendy that she can't hide. I'll be back." And, with that, he grabbed his buddy—who had remained silent this whole time—and pulled him along, and they stormed away.

She followed, so she could see their vehicle and luckily was fast enough to grab a photo. She didn't know that it would have caught the license plate, but it was good enough for her to at least see part of it.

With them gone, she returned to the store and faced Wendy. "Now, you should be okay for today. But they will be back."

Wendy paled and nodded. "What will you do with that picture?"

"I'll go talk to Mack," she said gently. "So you can expect to hear from him later today."

Wendy started to wring her hands.

"Have you done anything wrong?" Doreen asked immediately.

Wendy shook her head. "No, no, of course not."

"Then don't worry about it," she stated. "We can't have these guys coming back here to give you a shakedown over and over." As she walked to the front door with her animals, ready to leave, she turned back, looked at Wendy, and asked,

"By the way, what was the item that the woman was trying to sell?"

An odd look crossed Wendy's face. "It was a ring, with a big yellow stone. I thought it was fake at first, and, while I … I kind of admired it, it was truly awful, big, and gaudy. Then she said she wanted ten grand for it." Wendy laughed. "And whether it was fake or not, that woman clearly thought it real, and she had to be nuts to think I had that kind of money lying around."

"A real or fake what though?"

"A yellow diamond," she replied. "Supposedly one of the biggest yellow diamonds in the world. She said something about having heard that I'd found and sold a similar one about ten years ago."

"And did you?"

"No way. I don't handle jewelry, other than some occasional costume pieces that may come in. Besides, I don't have anything like that kind of money to be even paying for an appraisal, much less buying expensive diamonds like that. And it certainly wasn't my personal style."

The thing about rings was, they were very personal. Doreen had seen many rings that she would have called fake and gaudy looking on the hands of women who were millionaires. "And what happened to the ring this woman brought with her?"

"She disappeared with it," Wendy told Doreen, raising both hands. "And I don't even know who she was."

"Do you remember what she looks like?"

She shook her head. "No. Sunglasses, big hat, a big coat, collar turned up, said she had laryngitis, so she spoke in a whisper," she explained. "I didn't even consider all that as suspicious, until I saw the ring. I was thinking, you know, costume jewelry. And this woman was thinking I was a millionaire." Wendy gave a bitter laugh. "I should have just told her not to bother even walking through my store. But I didn't. Now look what happened."

Chapter 3

D OREEN WALKED SLOWLY home, realizing another disadvantage of having her pets with her was she couldn't get into the bank with them all either. But she had managed to get to the machine and put the check in. Something she wasn't terribly comfortable with still, but, because Doreen knew that Wendy was likely good for it—although who knew for sure, given what she'd just gone through—Doreen would be on tenterhooks for the next two days, waiting for the check to clear.

Once back home again she put on another piece of toast, checked out the fridge, and winced. The last little bit of cheese could go on her toast, and the last tomato would probably be sliced up for lunch, and maybe peanut butter would be her dinner, if... And she walked over to her pantry, opened up the door, and spied the last of her peanut butter. "Wow, we got paid just in time."

She checked on the animals' food supply, and they all had plenty. But she was concerned that there wasn't a whole lot left for her. If Mack saw how empty her fridge was, he'd get quite angry with her again. And she hadn't been paid for the gardening yet that she'd done on Sunday, but she knew that, as soon as she saw him again, he would pay her. And there'd be enough for some basics for her, but it sure wouldn't be more than that.

She left Mack a message to call her, so she could update him on Wendy's problem and also to share her photo of the goons' big white van. Yet she missed his return call, and he left her a message, not saying a whole lot. She figured he had his head in a case—and so did she. Doreen headed out with the animals for another walk. Several things bothered her about those thugs at Wendy's store. Where had the vehicle gone? Why had they focused on Wendy? And what could possibly have happened to that ring?

If any security cameras were on the nearby streets, then maybe Mack could follow the goons' exit pathway, possibly trailing the guys home even. But, according to Wendy, the guys bothering her stated the woman didn't have the yellow diamond when they found her. So what were the chances that this woman had stashed it somewhere between Wendy's store and wherever she was going? Or, considering the number of items in Wendy's store, what were the chances that maybe the unknown woman had stashed the ring in some clothing on display? Many of those garments in Wendy's store had pockets. Plus, Wendy carried a good selection of purses too.

On impulse, Doreen picked up her phone and called Wendy.

When Wendy heard her voice, she asked, "Did you talk to Mack?"

"I've left messages," she replied. "Is there any chance that woman hid that item in your inventory as she left?"

"I don't think so," she noted. "Yet I remember how she went out the back door."

"Why would she have done that?"

"Because people were coming in the front. I thought she went out the front door initially, but I realized then, after you left, that I'm pretty sure she went out the rear door. I don't know where she went after that."

"And you had cameras back then?"

"Yes, but I hadn't downloaded anything from them, and, when the guys showed up, they destroyed the cameras anyway. I … I can't get anything off them."

"Right." Doreen nodded. "Maybe I'll take a walk around the back of your store soon and just see if she could have stashed it somewhere outside."

"Do you think she did?" Wendy asked hopefully.

"I'm not sure," Doreen admitted. "We should be prepared for the fact that the ring was possibly stolen and that she may have stolen it from the thieves or that she's the thief and that those goons were the ones who owned it—or, more likely, they were all involved in stealing it together, and she's now stolen it from them. Or alternatively," she added, "and I do have personal experience with this, she's a woman trying to leave her husband, and that's the only thing she could take to start a new life."

At that, Wendy snorted. "You know what? You should start writing fiction because most of what you just suggested is what nobody would have thought of."

"Ha," Doreen muttered. "Anyway, don't be surprised if you see me down and around the back today. I'll … I'm coming your direction anyway. I had planned to check the front of the store, but if you say she went out the back …"

"I think she did," Wendy repeated. "She darted out, saw customers coming, darted back in, and asked if she could go out the back, so went out that way."

"Right. How are you feeling right now?"

"Nervous," Wendy admitted. "I don't know quite what's going on."

"Got it," Doreen agreed. "Let me take a look, and we'll see what we can come up with."

And, with that, she gathered her animals again, and all of them headed to Wendy's alleyway. Mugs acted like it had been forever since she had taken him for a walk. "Hey, we were just outside, walking the whole way to Wendy's, not ninety minutes ago. Sheesh." Even Goliath gave her a glare. "Stop your complaining. We are all outside. *Again*. You act like I'm mistreating you."

Thaddeus chimed in. "Thaddeus loves Doreen. Thaddeus loves Doreen."

"Ah, thank you, Thaddeus. It's nice to know you appreciate and love me. I love you too." With a flick of Goliath's tail and a tug from Mugs for Doreen to hurry up, she sighed. "And I love Mugs and Goliath too, even though they are acting snippy today for some reason."

Once they all arrived at Wendy's shop, Doreen wandered up and down the alleyway, as her mind tried to figure out exactly what somebody would do back here—who didn't want to be caught—yet was hanging on to a large diamond. If there was a chance that woman would get caught by those goons, then surely she would want to hide the ring close by, so she could return and retrieve it again.

But what if you were trying to get away from these people and didn't think that those goons would let you live? At that thought, she winced because, of course, now she sounded like she was writing a thriller. But, at the same time, she definitely noted some validity to her hypothesis.

She wandered from the top of the alley all the way down

the back, passing by some dumpsters, considering how those wouldn't make it easy for retrieval either. Chances are the woman—if she had put something like that ring in a dumpster—would have expected to come right back or was trying to get rid of the ring permanently, so that nobody would have it.

Pondering that, Doreen headed to the little parking space behind Wendy's and searched. On the other side of the alley was a large fence and a bunch of fruit trees and maple trees and evergreens. It's possible that the woman had tossed the diamond over the fence, but again she'd have to remember where it was in order to pick it up again.

Something that valuable wasn't something you wanted to take a chance of losing. However, if she feared that the goons were closing in on her, and she would soon be caught, and thinking for sure that they would never let her keep it, and maybe how she didn't want it to fall into the wrong hands, well, she might have just tossed it over a fence, thinking it was better to come back and even not find it than to get caught with it. Particularly if nobody knew or could prove that she had had it to begin with.

With all these different things running around in her head, Doreen walked up and down the alleyway several times, and finally, when she turned and walked back, she found Wendy, standing at her open back door.

"Well?" she asked.

Doreen shrugged. "I'm not sure that I see anything suspicious at all. Yet I do see so many options but nothing concrete."

"That's what I thought too," Wendy agreed.

Just then a murder of crows came and landed on the dumpster beside her. "How long have the crows been around here?" Doreen asked.

When a crow cawed at her, Thaddeus poked his head out from under Doreen's long hair and cawed back. That set up a cacophony of conversation that was so loud, it was almost impossible to hear herself think, since Thaddeus sat on her neck by her right ear. Finally she calmed him down, and the crows took off.

She looked at Thaddeus. "Well, the least you could have done was ask them if they had seen something shiny and yellow," she muttered.

"Thaddeus loves Doreen," Thaddeus replied.

"Yeah, I get that." She chuckled. "Still doesn't mean that you can't be a help too."

Wendy stared in fascination. "He really does talk, doesn't he?"

"He really does," she replied. "Sometimes too much. And he does definitely like to see other birds around." Doreen sighed. "I never realized that he may be missing his feathered friends."

"But crows don't talk."

"Well, I'm not so sure about that," Doreen stated. "I have heard that, besides being incredibly intelligent, some crows have learned to mimic sounds."

"And yet Thaddeus seems to do more than mimicking sounds."

She nodded. "I would say he's definitely communicating. Whether he theoretically understands what he's saying, that, of course, is up for debate." She gently rubbed her head back and forth along Thaddeus's feathers, cuddling the bird that she was so attached to.

"It is pretty fascinating how quickly the two of you have developed a bond."

"And I think maybe that's because Nan had already approved me as the *replacement Thaddeus slave*," she explained, with a chuckle.

Wendy laughed. "No, I think you share a real bond there. Maybe being the slave to a bird is how it might have started, but he cares about you."

"I know he does," she murmured, gently stroking his beak. "He's very special." Then she looked back to where the crows had been at the dumpster. She asked, "When's the garbage picked up?"

"Every Monday," Wendy stated. "Why?"

"And how long ago was this woman here?"

"Ah, you mean, has the dumpster been emptied since that woman was here? Yes. She was here a couple weeks ago."

"And how often do the goons come by and visit?"

"Too often," she stated. "I don't know what they think they can do."

"Well, that'd be one of the questions that we get to ask them," she noted. "The fact of the matter is, you don't have the ring, and they need to let that go."

"I think it's too much money for them to let go of the idea of finding that ring," she admitted quietly.

"Yeah, I bet you're right, and the question is whether or not the money or the ring is actually theirs."

Chapter 4

INTENDING TO RETURN home once again, Doreen stopped at the end of Wendy's alleyway, checking out a tree that she hadn't seen in a very long time. She took a picture of the fruit, when a woman on the other side of the fence said, "Hey, are you stealing my quince?"

"Oh my," Doreen said, as she tried to stand tall enough so she could see over the fence and could see the woman on the other side. "I took a picture of it," she admitted. "It's beautiful. I haven't seen a quince tree in a very long time." Since she couldn't see over the six-foot-tall fence, Doreen found a better view through a gap in the wooden fence.

"They're not common anymore," the older lady replied.

She wandered toward Doreen using a cane, her legs more bowed than anything. It was amazing that she could even walk, as both knees seemed to go in opposite directions. This was probably Esther, who Mack had mentioned was the lady with the quince jam.

"But that tree's been here for almost as long as I have."

"Wow," she muttered. "And it's in such great health."

"Unlike me." The other woman gave a cackle. "But then I'm ninety-five years old, so I have a right to not be doing so great."

"I'm so sorry if you're struggling," Doreen noted gently. "It is a beautiful tree."

As she went to back up, the woman asked, "What's on your shoulder?"

Thaddeus stood tall and now peered over the fence.

"Oh, this is Thaddeus, my African Grey parrot."

"You have a parrot on your shoulder?" The woman seemed fascinated with the idea.

"Well, he is a pet," Doreen explained.

"Why doesn't he fly away?"

"He doesn't fly well to begin with," she noted, "and we're friends."

The woman stared at her for a long moment. "You know that, in my day, we probably would have considered it a pest."

"You mean, like the crows?"

"A murder of crows is always around here," the woman noted, shaking her head. "If I had a BB gun, I'd have taken them out a long time ago," she muttered. "Making a mess of everything, stealing everything."

"Do they come into your yard and take stuff?"

"If I drop something and leave it in the yard, they sure do," she noted. "You have to clean up behind you. Otherwise they steal everything."

"Well, that's kind of a cleaning up too, isn't it?"

"I suppose," she grumbled, "but they'll get at the quince as well. It always blows me away that every critter in this world knows when my fruit trees are full of ripe fruit, just ready for harvesting, and *bang*, I've got ants. I've got raccoons. I've got birds. All of them just taking off with my hard-earned fruit."

"I'm sorry," Doreen replied. "It would be nice if they at least shared."

"Well, they have their version of sharing versus my version of sharing," she noted, and then she laughed. "And who am I kidding? At my age I can't be climbing the trees nor be bothered making jams and jellies anymore anyway. And nobody left to eat them."

"Is that what you do with the quince?" Doreen asked, looking up at the tree. "This tree's much bigger than I thought."

"And it's just because it's so old," she stated. "It's had branches break a couple times over the years, but it always sprouts fresh and young again. Too bad people don't do that."

Looking again at the woman's crippled legs, Doreen nodded. "Wouldn't that be nice," she said gently. "And do you live here alone?"

The woman gave her a sharp look. "Sure do. No nursing home for me. At least not yet."

"Not while you can still look after yourself, I presume."

The woman cackled. "Exactly," she replied. "Some old folks' homes are around here, but I wouldn't want to go into any of them."

"I'm only familiar with Rosemoor," she admitted. "My grandmother lives there."

She looked at her and nodded. "That's where I know you from."

Doreen stared at Esther in surprise. "You know me?"

"Well, it depends. Do you have a dog and a cat at your feet?"

At that, Mugs barked several times.

The older woman moved down the fence, and, hearing a

noise, Doreen saw a gate open up nearby. And there was Esther, leaning heavily on the gate frame. "It is you," she added, but this time there was more delight than suspicion in her words. "You're the one who solves all those mysteries."

Even as the older woman looked on in delight, the murder of crows flew in to land on the quince tree above them. Esther immediately whacked the tree with her walking stick, trying to chase them away. Then she turned to glare at Doreen and saw the smile on her face. Doreen immediately wiped it off.

"Sorry," she replied. "I guess they're quite the pest, aren't they?"

Esther shrugged. "Whatever. I guess." She turned and looked back at Doreen and stated, "And, if you're bored, you might as well solve another mystery round there."

"Oh, what's that?"

"Somebody has been dumping my garbage," she declared, with a snarl. "And that's really irritating."

"Probably raccoons," Doreen guessed.

The woman stopped and looked at her with a side-eye glance. "Gee, I didn't think of that myself," she muttered sarcastically.

Doreen winced. "Have you watched anybody or seen anybody hanging around? Do you have any cameras around the place?"

"No, I don't have any cameras." She waved her hand about but didn't bother to turn around. "I've lived here all my life," she explained. "Haven't needed cameras, and the occasional bear has run by and the occasional raccoons too, but generally they leave my place alone. But now, two out of three nights, my garbage has been dumped. Like two weeks ago. So I don't even put it out anymore. I take it out now on the morning of the trash pickup, so I don't have to worry about it. But that means the smell collects in the house," she added. "Hate it."

"Where does your garbage bin go for collection?"

The woman turned, looked at her, and then pointed toward the alleyway. "It goes out where you're standing every Monday."

At that, Doreen nodded. "And you put the garbage out every Monday morning?"

The woman nodded. "I do now," she replied, "but don't worry about an old lady and her headache." She shook her head. "I'm sure you got something much more constructive to do."

Not knowing if that was sarcasm again or not, Doreen watched as this interesting character walked inside her fence and slammed the gate closed on her.

"Have a nice day," Doreen called over the fence. She heard just a *harrumph* on the other side. "You might enjoy Rosemoor," she added, not sure why she brought it up. Obviously the older lady didn't want to talk to her.

At that the other woman cackled. "Not likely. People die there." And, with that, she went into her house, and Doreen heard the door slam shut.

It was hard to argue with that philosophy. As Doreen had found out too, a lot of people died at Rosemoor, not all of them in a good way. But she could hardly hold the entire center at fault for that. Besides, her grandmother absolutely adored being there. But it did worry Doreen, after Peggy had killed Chrissy, that maybe Nan's life was in danger.

And, on that note, Doreen called her grandmother as she and her animals walked back toward home. "You up for a visit?" she asked.

"Always," replied her grandmother gaily through the phone. "Hopefully you've got the animals with you."

"Yep, we've done a lot of walking today," she noted, "so we're a little tired."

"I've got the tea on," she replied, "and treats for everyone."

Chapter 5

AND, WITH THAT, Doreen smiled and told Nan, "We'll be there in a little bit."

It took a little longer to get there than normal, but Doreen wasn't in any rush, and she was a little more tired today. But then you know? A couple pieces of toast, a little bit of cheese, and the last of the peanut butter didn't go a long way in terms of energy production in her body. And she couldn't really buy any groceries until that check cleared. She didn't have the money for the gardening yet either.

She finally made it to the Rosemoor parking lot, and the animals pulled her eagerly toward Nan. Doreen dropped Mugs's leash, and Mugs raced ahead to find Nan on the patio, waiting for him. She crouched down and gave him a big welcome, as he barked and danced all around her. She looked up, smiling, to find Goliath standing completely disinterested on her flower box, but his tail twitched, until Nan walked over and gave him a cuddle too.

When Thaddeus and Doreen finally stepped onto the patio, Nan said, "It is so lovely to see you."

Doreen bent down and gave her grandmother a hug. "And you too. How are you feeling?"

"Ah, I'm fine. You know that," she replied.

"Well, I know that you're fine now," she noted, "but you did give me a scare recently."

"Yes, something that you have given me lots of times." She arched a brow at her granddaughter.

Doreen laughed. "Very true. Very true. But, hey, I didn't get attacked on the last case."

"No, I noticed that," she stated. "I'm sure that made Mack happy."

She flushed at that. "He did mention something about it." She chuckled. "Finally."

"And it seems like you're a little more comfortable with the fact that he cares."

"I'm working my way toward it," Doreen admitted. "But I've also warned him that I need the divorce taken care of before I go too much further."

"Ha," Nan replied. "You know what? The sooner you go further, the divorce will matter less and less."

"I don't know about that," Doreen argued. "I want to get divorced, so that I am legally and emotionally free."

"Right, we're back to all those lovely morals and ethics and things that get in the way of a fun time." Nan laughed. "Tea's ready. I don't suppose you ate, did you? Because I stole a few treats from the kitchen."

"Nan, you're not supposed to do that. Remember?"

"I know, but I can't resist. They're so good."

"So did you steal them for you because that's allowed?"

"Well, I did," she declared. "I just stole so many that I can't eat them all," she explained craftily.

Doreen rolled her eyes at that but then gasped, as Nan pulled away the tea towel covering two baskets and exposed many little pies. "What are these?"

"They're meat pies," Nan stated, grinning broadly.

"And these two?" Doreen asked, as she pointed to a second basket.

"Dessert pies. I got a peach and an apple. But these? These are chicken pot pies, homemade in the kitchen. So I brought you two. Didn't know if you would eat them both now or maybe take one home later."

"But what about you?" she asked.

"I've already had three." She laughed, placing her hand to her tummy.

She had said it in such a guilty tone that Doreen had to chuckle.

"They are so good," Nan added.

"Well, I'm thrilled for you," she murmured. "And for me." She sat down, with the animals gathered around them. Mugs, now sensing that maybe some treats were on offer for him, stood up on his back legs to sniff the table. "No, you don't," she told him. "I get to eat these. You have lots of dog food at home. I'm the one who doesn't."

"Why would you want to eat dog food at home?" Nan asked, looking at her in horror.

Doreen shook her head. "That's not what I meant."

"I hope not," Nan muttered, frowning at her. "You're not that broke, are you?"

"*That* broke? No, I'm just the regular kind of broke," she replied, "but not to the point of having to eat dog food yet."

"Don't say *yet*," Nan replied. "That's never a good thing."

"No, maybe not." Doreen laughed.

Meanwhile Nan got up and brought back treats for the animals. They were all happy to see that.

"I can't say that I would be thrilled at having to eat dog

food. I did get a check from Wendy today, and I got it in the bank, but I'll have to wait a couple days for it to clear."

Nan nodded. "I never had to worry about that. I always had money in the bank account to cover it."

"Sure," Doreen admitted, "but, if it doesn't clear, I'm really in trouble."

"Right," Nan agreed. "And I guess you have all your utilities to pay, don't you?" Nan shook her head. "It's nice that Rosemoor takes care of that here."

She nodded. "Yes. Paying bills is kind of a pain."

Nan chuckled. "But it's nice to have an electric washing machine and a fridge and all the other good things that make life easier, more convenient," she noted.

"I know. I know. And it's silly because those conveniences are definitely something that I really do enjoy having. But having to pay for it? Well, I can't say I enjoy that part too much."

Nan chuckled. "No, I get it," she stated, "but, hey, you're doing so well on your own."

"Maybe."

At that, Nan popped up. "Let me go grab the teapot. I made tea too." And she disappeared inside.

Doreen picked up one of the meat pies closest to her and took a sniff. It smelled absolutely divine. And almost immediately her stomach growled.

As Nan returned, she said, "Eat, child, eat."

Doreen looked at her. "I was waiting for you."

"Oh, don't, don't." Nan waved her hand about. "I'm not eating anyway, and you should never stand on manners here," she added.

Doreen never really understood what that phrase meant, but she was quite happy to take a bite. As she bit into it, juice dribbled down her chin. She snatched a napkin and dabbed at her chin. "My, that's delicious."

"Isn't it?" Nan crowed. "I'm always happy to have them try new things here, but, wow, this has been such a great experiment."

"No, you're right," Doreen agreed. She quickly polished off the first one and then gave a happy sigh, as she sat back. "You know what? That was truly delicious."

"Well then, eat the second one."

"I think I'd rather take it home and eat it later," she murmured, "if that's okay with you?"

"Absolutely it is," she noted. "Besides, you can have a dessert one now too."

She chuckled and watched as Nan poured tea. As soon as there was tea, she picked up a dessert pie and sniffed it. "Oh my, this smells so good."

"Yep, it sure does. And it tastes just as nice."

"You're lucky that Rosemoor cooks for the residents but also that you have your own kitchen too, so you can bake and cook when you want to as well. And you get to bring food back to your apartment," she added. "Then you have snacks for later."

"Not that I need them," Nan noted. "When you think about it, I have a lot of meals here already taken care of that I don't need to store food for later, but sometimes it's … Sometimes I don't feel like going down to the dining room, or I just want to have a bit of time alone," she explained. "And, in that case, it's always nice to have a bite in my apartment."

"And can you go down at dinnertime and take a plate back?"

"They don't really like it, but, yes, we can." She smirked,

and then she shrugged. "The food here is great, but, when they do something like this, well, you know a few of us might pick up a little bit extra and share."

"Of course you do." Doreen chuckled. She took a bite and realized that she had the peach one. "Wow," she mumbled, as the full flavor hit her. "This is beautiful. The peaches taste so fresh. And this is a real homemade crust. Just wonderful."

"I think so too." Nan grinned. "Now you can see how I could eat so many of them that I felt sick." At that, she nudged her teacup closer to Doreen.

Doreen obligingly picked it up, had a sip, and took another bite. By the time she was done eating, she sat back and finished off her cup of tea. "You know I don't come here just to eat."

Nan laughed. "That's good"—she nodded—"because lots of times we don't have food for you. So it's a good thing ... that's not why you come."

She laughed. "Absolutely it's not why I come. I come to see you."

"And you got a check from Wendy, so that's huge too."

"Yes, thankfully," she noted. "I can pay off those utility bills sitting there, nagging at me, and get a few groceries." But she frowned at that because, of course, now that she had remembered she had the utility bills to pay as well, she wasn't sure how much money she actually had left for groceries. She sighed. "It would be nice to get some of that auction money in."

"It's coming," Nan stated. "It really is."

"I suppose," Doreen agreed reluctantly. "It just ... it's taking its sweet time."

At that, Nan snorted. "Anytime you're waiting for something, it always takes forever. And, if you didn't need it and if you didn't care, it would be there in a heartbeat."

"Well, I certainly won't try to make it look like I don't care," she replied, laughing, "because, of course, it … it does matter. And, you know, groceries are a little thin on the ground right now."

At that, Nan looked at her in surprise. "You are eating, aren't you?" she demanded.

"Sure," Doreen agreed. "You just gave me food."

Nan frowned at that. "I did, but I didn't give you very much." Then she stopped, looked down at the rest of the pot pies, and noted, "And you're much taller than I am, so you need a lot more food."

"I'm fine," Doreen replied. "You just gave me a wonderful treat, and I have two to go home with."

Nan settled back at that. "I do worry about you."

"And I worry about you," she added. "I spoke to an older lady today who knew you and me."

"Who's that?"

Doreen explained the location and described the older lady.

"I'm not sure who you mean," Nan admitted. "I did know one woman down there." She thought about it. "Esther, maybe?" she guessed. "I'm not sure. Esther's quite a bit older than me. You said that this woman was ninety-five?"

At that, Doreen nodded. "Something like that."

"That makes her quite a bit older than me." Nan sniffed and gave a gentle pat to her hair. "But some characters are around this town who, of course, I might have brushed up against in my last twenty, thirty years," she explained delicately.

"She definitely knew you. Although she didn't appear to be angry at you, so I'll take that as a good sign."

Nan chuckled. "What about a husband?"

"She didn't say anything about that. Just that somebody was getting into her garbage all the time lately, and it's really a pain."

She looked at her in surprise. "Why would anybody want to go through her garbage?"

At that, Doreen sat back and shrugged. "You know what? That's a really good question. I don't imagine she cooks much and probably doesn't have a whole lot of leftovers."

"And that means you're thinking it's an animal."

"Why wouldn't it be animal?" she asked, looking at her grandmother, puzzled.

"I mean, are you thinking that somebody around there might think she has something of value?"

"I don't know, not sure what I'm thinking it was to begin with."

"Okay, now you've got me really curious." Nan leaned in closer. "Can you describe her again?" When Doreen gave her a bit of information on the woman's height this time and explained about her knees, Nan exclaimed, "It is Esther, the quince jam lady. She was supposed to have knee operations, but something went wrong with the surgery. Her doctor said it was something to do with the cartilage in her knees, but her legs started to bow out really badly after that. She walks with a cane?"

Or two. At that, Doreen nodded.

"Yep, that's Esther. She used to be a silver worker too," she added. "She made some pretty incredible jewelry in her time."

"That's interesting," Doreen noted, "but it still doesn't explain why anybody would be worried about her garbage."

"No. *Hmm.*" Nan thought about it, shrugged, and then stated, "I'm not really sure why either." Nan frowned at Doreen. "Did you ask her about what was in her garbage?"

"No, I didn't." Doreen shook her head. "It did seem kind of impertinent, especially when she was already quite upset about it. She has this beautiful quince tree in her backyard."

"Ah, now you've clinched it for sure," Nan stated. "I adore her quince jam. It is to die for. A long time ago she used to take it to the market. She makes the best quince jam in town." She nodded. "Beyond town even. I'm not sure anybody else makes it like she does."

"She didn't sound like she made it very much anymore, and she told me that the birds were attacking her fruit trees pretty routinely."

"Well, in the olden days, she would have been out there with a BB gun probably, knocking off the birds," she explained. "Esther was a bit of a terror."

"I'm sure she was," Doreen agreed, with a smirk. "She still looks like a bit of a terror."

"Yeah, not somebody you want to cross in the dark," Nan muttered, "although I'm sure she's slowed down some now."

"She definitely has at that," Doreen agreed. Then she held up one finger and asked, "Do you know anybody in town who would be wealthy enough to have a big yellow diamond ring?"

"Wow, that's a change of conversation."

Doreen flushed. "I was just wondering about it."

"No, you weren't," Nan declared. Then she leaned forward and whispered, "You're on a new case."

"Maybe," Doreen noted cautiously, "but I can't give you any details yet."

At that, her grandmother sat back, disappointed, but her gaze was intent as it studied Doreen's. "Are you sure about that? I might be a help."

"Maybe. And maybe you can't because you don't know anybody who has that kind of money."

"Yellow diamonds aren't necessarily that expensive," Nan argued. Then she frowned and added, "Who am I kidding? I mean, if it's of any big size, it could be worth millions."

"Well, that's the question," Doreen noted, "and who in town would have one?"

Nan frowned. "Some of the wealthiest people in Canada live here in Kelowna," she stated. "And a lot of wealthy people retire here, and you wouldn't know who they are because they've been here for so long that they live cheerfully modestly, without letting anybody know they have that kind of money."

"Which is a good way to do it," Doreen suggested.

"Maybe. But, at the same time, a lot of major property developers are here, so a lot of rich developers' wives are here too. Plus we have a lot of wineries in town. So it could be any number of people."

Doreen didn't know what to say to that. "Particularly if it was a large solitaire," she mumbled.

At that, Nan's gaze widened. "What did you say?" she asked in a hoarse whisper. She leaned forward. "Are you talking like an engagement ring?"

"Maybe. Why?"

"Because one was stolen." Her fingers rapped on the tabletop. "But I can't remember when or from whom."

"What do you mean, from whom? Did you know who lost one?"

"No, not yet. I'm trying to remember the details," Nan admitted. "I remember hearing about it, but it was quite a few years ago now."

"Interesting," Doreen replied. "And now the questions are, who would have stolen it, and would the police know about it?"

"I'm sure the police have a file on it," Nan confirmed. "It was a big media circus at the time. I think it was some …" She stopped and stared off in space. "You know what? I think it was a young trophy wife to one of the big executives who owns one of the big development companies in town. He was engaged to some sweet young thing, and she had insisted on a ring, a big showy ring. And that's the one she sported."

"Interesting. Did they ever get married?"

"You know what? I'm not sure that they did." Nan stopped, staring at Doreen. "I don't follow the gossip column very much anymore."

"And you never heard anything else about the fate of the ring?"

She shook her head. "No, I never did."

"Interesting that you brought it up though."

"Sure," Nan agreed, "but you also know that I could have had a lot of reasons for knowing about it. I'm sure I took all kinds of bets on that case."

"Isn't that the truth?" Doreen said, with a heavy sigh. "Well, now you've given me something to think about. Too bad you didn't give me a solution to it as well."

"You're sure you can't tell me even a little bit on this

new case of yours?"

"I've already told you a little bit," Doreen stated, "and don't mention it to anybody else."

At that, Nan's eyes widened. "Ooh, so it really is secret."

"It is secret," Doreen confirmed. "I just need to keep you safe and to keep me safe and to keep somebody else safe."

Nan drew her hand across her lips, as if zipping a zipper. "I won't tell anyone."

Doreen rolled her eyes at that. "I'm serious, Nan, not even Richie."

"I promise," Nan replied. "But you will fill me in, won't you?"

"Sure. And, if you think of anything else that goes along with this case, let me know. Particularly the names."

"Names, names, names," she repeated, then sat up taller. "*Bernard.* I think that was the name of the guy who was engaged. But I can't remember what his girlfriend's name was, although that's a name I should remember because, as I recall, it was pretty stupid."

"What do you mean by stupid?"

"You know, when you think about a stripper or something like that, and you hear all those names that sound like make-believe, hers was like one of those."

"You mean, like Candy or something?" Doreen asked curiously.

"You know what? I think it was like Candy."

Doreen stared at her grandmother in surprise. "Obviously that wasn't her real name."

"Maybe it was," Nan noted, with an eye roll, "but that's what he called her."

"Well, I don't think I'll get very close to him to ask him about the state of that ring, but it would be interesting if I could do some searches on that name."

"Not that name," Nan added, "but something close to it."

"I've got a phone call into Mack," Doreen shared. "Maybe he'll remember something."

"It was before his time here, I'm sure," Nan noted. "So maybe it was longer than ten years ago." She sighed. "I don't know where the years all went, but they just seemed to disappear when I wasn't looking."

Doreen laughed. "I think half the world would say that."

"Maybe. It is sad though."

"Sure it's sad, but let's enjoy every day that we have, while we have it," Doreen stated. "As you and I both know, those days can run by too fast, and suddenly we're out of days to even enjoy." Doreen paused, before asking Nan, "How are you handling the Chrissy thing now?"

"I feel guilty and sad," she admitted. "I feel like I let her down, but I'm working on it. And, of course, Peggy is gone, and now we have this new cook." She stared at the baskets of small individual pies, rubbing her hands in delight. "That's a huge gift. So we all thank you for that one."

At that, Doreen shook her head. "You can't thank me for that. I haven't done anything yet."

"But you did. You got rid of Peggy. And, although we didn't have a known problem with Peggy back then, we do much prefer our new cook."

"And let's hope this one doesn't feel like killing any of the residents."

She chuckled. "I don't think so. She's young and trying to make a name."

"Interesting that she's here then."

Nan looked at her and then slowly nodded. "I didn't

even think of that. Ha, maybe we have a mystery after all."

"And maybe you don't," Doreen interjected, afraid her grandmother was up to resuming her betting activities. Doreen slowly stood, rubbed her tummy, and said, "Thank you for the treats."

Nan immediately got up, grabbed the small bag that Doreen hadn't even noticed sitting on the side, put two pot pies inside—one meat and one apple—and handed the bag over to her. "Here. Enjoy those tonight."

"I will," Doreen agreed, snatching the bag eagerly. She leaned over, kissed Nan on the cheek, and replied, "Now you have a good evening."

"I will."

And, with that, Doreen turned and gathered her animals and headed back home.

Chapter 6

Tuesday Morning

THE NEXT MORNING, before 8:00 a.m., she sat on the deck, still trying to wake up, when she heard a man at the front door, calling out to her. Immediately Mugs, barking and barking and barking, raced toward Mack, standing at the front door.

She called back, "I'm in the backyard." When she turned, he came toward her, carrying a cup of coffee in his hand. She looked at him and smiled.

"Hey," he said, "you look tired."

"Didn't sleep all that well last night," she replied, "too many thoughts running around in my head."

"Doesn't sound like good thoughts either," he noted. "Problems?"

"Did you get my messages?"

He nodded. "That's why I'm here. I ended up on another case last night and didn't get much sleep either."

"Sorry," she apologized. "I always have to remind myself that you're busy and have a job to do."

He shrugged. "Normally wouldn't be so bad but we're also very short-staffed, so yesterday was just one of those days. I got to bed at midnight. So tell me what Wendy shared with you."

Doreen quickly explained. He interrupted her several times for more details. By the time she fell silent, he just stared at her.

"So you thought that you should confront these two guys in the back of her store, for what reason?"

"Because she was terrified. They needed to know that she wasn't alone."

"But did you give them the impression that she wasn't alone or just that she wasn't there that day?"

"Just that she wasn't there that day," she admitted, "but she did need a break, and she does need someone standing with her."

"Got it," he noted. "And how absolutely fascinating that a large yellow diamond gets mentioned."

"Why?"

"Because, of course, your second message."

She winced. "Right. Yeah. I forgot about that."

"You forgot about it?"

"Mack, I need all the information you can get me on a yellow diamond theft from over ten years ago."

And he shook his head and glared at her. "You know I am busy, right?"

"I know," she admitted gently. "I also didn't bug you to get back to me on the double either. I knew that you would get here when you could, but what else could I do? If I start looking in all kinds of secret places, it'll piss you off."

He sighed. "What do you mean, *secret places*?"

"I have some sources," she noted. "I am heading to the library this morning to see what I could come up with on the various personalities involved, but I didn't have a whole lot to go on as far as searching for somebody named Candy."

"Yeah, that's because her name is Cassandra Yoloft."

"Oh. Did they ever get married?"

"Nope, sure didn't. There was a big brouhaha about the theft. He accused her of stealing it. She accused him of stealing it. Things got ugly. They couldn't see their way to the altar after that."

"Gee, I wonder why?" she quipped. "Sounds like they weren't exactly meant for each other."

"Let's just say he decided he didn't need to marry her. He'd already lost a very expensive ring."

"And did he have that kind of money?" she asked dubiously. "I mean, I get it. He's in business and all, and I know that we have more billionaires now heading into trillionaires here in Kelowna. But still, really?"

Mack sighed. "There was some story about that ring itself too. Matter of fact, it's got a lot of mystery to it."

"How am I only just hearing about this now?" she complained.

"It's a burglary." Mack shrugged. "What do you want me to say? At the time it was assumed that Cassandra—or Candy, as you know her—took off with it."

"And yet then suddenly it shows up."

"No," he corrected her. "Suddenly a yellow ring that may or may not look anything like the one in question shows up. According to Wendy. But we don't know what ring it was or whether it was even a genuine yellow diamond."

Doreen pondered that and then gave him marks for clarity. "No, you're right," she agreed. "But these two goons are after something, and they're pretty adamant about getting it."

"And yet, if Wendy doesn't have it, she doesn't have it."

"True, and that would explain why they haven't killed anyone yet," Doreen noted.

"Whoa, whoa, whoa, whoa. Nobody said anything about killing people."

"No, not yet." She slid him a look. "But you and I both know that, if these goons really think that doing so will get them that diamond, then her life's forfeited, all for greed."

"But we don't know that," he stated immediately. "We don't know anything like that."

She smiled. "No, we sure don't. But I like Wendy, and she still owes me money, so I don't want anything to happen to her."

He stared at her. "Seriously? That's your only reason?"

"I said I liked her first," she stated defensively. "Besides, any chance there's a reward if I do find the ring?"

His stare turned into a glare to which he added a frown. "You know something? There just might be. At least there was, but I don't know if it's still being offered."

Chapter 7

A S SOON AS Mack left, Doreen locked up her house, waved goodbye to her animals, and raced down to the library. Sometimes the internet gave her more information, but sometimes she had to get into the archives and just see what was there. Some background history on this Bernard person and anything she could find on Candy would be huge. As she walked into the library, the librarian looked up and sniffed.

Doreen gave her one of her most winning smiles. "Hey." She hesitated and added, "You know that I work on a lot of these older cases." The librarian looked at her in surprise and then slowly nodded. "So I'm now working on the missing yellow diamond from a good decade or so ago," she explained. "Apparently Bernard's fiancée had it stolen."

At that, the librarian looked at her and then chuckled. "I remember that. We all thought he was a fool for thinking he wanted to marry her in the first place." She grinned. "But there's no fool like an old fool, especially a rich man, who's looking for something bright and young on his arm."

"And in his bed," Doreen added in a dry tone.

At that, the librarian gave her a sober nod. "Very true. I

don't know that we have very much on it."

"Newspaper articles? Anything that may have been archived? Any court documents on anything?"

"I'll send you to the area where they would be," she stated, "but most of that stuff—because it was after the internet—should all be online."

"Sure, it should be, but then you and I both know that a lot of that stuff gets hard to find after a while."

The librarian pursed her lips, as she walked Doreen to the back corner, where stacks and stacks of newspapers were stored.

"And do we have all of these from years ago archived?" Doreen asked her.

"We do," the librarian confirmed. "We have three years here in actual paper copy, and then, if you go farther back, they're all over here." And she returned to where the archives were. "You can search as normal in here because it's just one big database." She stepped aside and added, "Yeah, good luck with that."

"You think it'll be a problem?" Doreen asked.

"Nobody's seen the diamond since it was stolen."

"Maybe not," Doreen admitted. "Then again somebody may have just seen it a couple weeks ago."

At that, the librarian turned and stared.

Doreen shrugged. "Like I said, I'm on it."

"Oh my." She smiled. "Did you actually see it?"

"Not yet," Doreen replied, "but I have hopes. I'm not sure there's anything quite like diamonds in this world."

"I would love to see it," the librarian noted eagerly. "Can you imagine?"

"I can't actually. It's not for me—that's for sure."

"Really?" The librarian seemed surprised.

She shrugged. "Yeah, I'm not so much into diamonds. Much more into finding the criminals who are behind stealing them."

"And yet," the librarian noted, "nobody died."

"Maybe not, but then again, how do we know that?"

The librarian looked at her and then smirked. "So, is this a case, or are you just, you know, bored?"

"It's a case," she confirmed, "but thanks for the vote of confidence. I have enough to do without digging into things that are of no value."

"If you say so." She turned and headed back to the front desk.

As soon as the librarian was out of sight, Doreen sat down at the archives and started searching through the names that she had. With a small notebook to jot down notes, she brought up whatever there was. When seeing some things that were of interest but not wanting to spend her time reading it all here, she quickly copied over a lot of the information and emailed it to herself.

When an hour had gone by, the librarian stopped by again and asked, "Did you find anything?"

"Not a whole lot, but I did find an official engagement announcement and a nice picture of the couple with that engagement ring front and center. Seems to have been the thing to do back then. Much less now I'd think," she muttered, as she stood and stretched. "I did run across a lot of conjecture about the loss of the ring. While many people were talking about it, not a whole lot of actual evidence was produced."

"If there were," the librarian stated, "I would think the police would have solved it by now."

Doreen didn't say anything to that because, of course, so

far, there wasn't a whole lot she could say. Sure the police would have solved it if they could have, but, as she had found, time and distance made a huge difference when it came to solving these old cases.

People had a tendency to keep quiet for a very long time, and then, all of a sudden, they no longer thought it was an issue or then maybe they tried to come clean to get out of some trouble that they were in, before they met their maker. Either way, she wouldn't sit here and talk about it. "Anyway, I'm done for now," Doreen declared. "Thank you." And, with that said, she quickly walked out of the library, notepad in hand, before the librarian could ask Doreen any more questions.

Outside she stopped and took a breath and reoriented herself as to what she would do next. What she did need were some groceries. Mack had paid her a few bucks for the gardening, so she had that in hand, and, without her animals, she could quickly go take care of what she needed. However, she also needed to know whether Wendy's check had cleared the bank. Considering that she needed to pay the utilities first, she would just grab a little bit of groceries for herself, using Mack's cash.

With that in mind, she drove to the grocery store and to the local farmers' market as well. As soon as she walked inside, she pulled out the money that Mack had given her, counted it, and realized it was more than she expected, more than what she got paid per visit. Then, as she thought about it, Mack hadn't paid her for the last time either, so this was technically for two days' worth of gardening time. So that was good.

Doreen quickly bought some salad greens, some fresh veggies, and then headed over and picked up several loaves of bread, a block of cheese again, and more peanut butter.

As she pondered her purchases, a woman behind her noted, "You can't live on that."

She turned to see the older lady, whom she had met behind Wendy's, now walking toward her, using two canes. Esther, according to Nan. Doreen frowned. "Don't you get grocery delivery?" she asked Esther. "Surely it's easier than getting out and walking."

"It's probably easier," Esther agreed, "but I don't have a whole lot of money, and even the delivery cost is prohibitive."

Hearing that, Doreen immediately was sympathetic. "I know. Can't say I have any money to waste either."

"If what you're buying is an example of the money you do have," she noted, "you'll starve."

"I hope not," Doreen replied, with a smile. "I've done okay for a while so far, and I do have money coming, but it's not here yet."

"Yeah, well, I don't know who owes you money, but that's what they all say. *The check's in the mail.*"

Realizing that Esther didn't understand Doreen's situation, and that was okay too, Doreen added, "I'm also not the world's best cook, so I'm learning how to deal with things."

"Well, if you have peanut butter, you should have jam."

"No, that's not in the budget," she admitted. "Peanut butter will keep me alive. Jam? Well, that's a whole different extravagance."

At that, the older woman reached out a gnarled hand, grabbed Doreen by the arm, and said, "You come to my place this afternoon." She wagged a finger in Doreen's face. "I've got lots of jam."

And Doreen remembered about Esther's quinces.

"Quince jam?" she asked hopefully, remembering Mack's and Nan's comments.

"Absolutely," she declared. "Do you like it?"

"I love it," she said honestly. "I just haven't had it in a very long time. I used to get a random taste of it from Nan, when I visited her as a child."

"And that was my quinces," she stated, chuckling. "I sold her more than a few jars over the years. Didn't realize they were going to you."

Doreen shook her head. "Not jars. Just some tastes here and there went to me. Whenever I was lucky enough to visit my grandmother. Nan loved your quince jam so much.'

"Well, that's good. I'm glad that you and your grandmother are close."

"We are," she replied immediately. "It's hard watching her age, as the years reach out and choke the life out of people." Doreen raised one hand. "Nan is still doing very well—don't get me wrong—but I recognize when somebody is getting older, and that just makes it hard to see."

At that the older lady looked at her and nodded. "Very true. And I mean it. Come by this afternoon. I've got all kinds of canned stuff I'll never eat."

"And yet you would save all kinds of money if you did."

"Sure," she admitted, "but I think I was putting aside for a winter day, but not just a day. Turns out I was putting aside for decades of winters," she shared. "So come on by. I'll expect you." She looked at her watch. "I'll see you in about an hour and a half." And, with that, she turned and toddled off slowly.

Doreen wasn't sure what to make of it. As much as she would love some quince jam, she wasn't so sure about any old canning that she didn't know more about. She didn't even know how safe some of that at-home canning stuff was. But she figured that it might be worth going down there to at least get the jam. Although how to refuse anything else was a bit of a challenge.

As she quickly went through the cash-only lane with her few items, she noted the cashier looking at her strangely.

Doreen gave her a bland look, smiled, and asked, "You having a good day?"

The other woman just nodded and asked her, "Are you?"

"Sure," Doreen replied, "I just needed to pick up a few staples to go with all my fresh stuff." The woman shrugged and didn't say anything, and Doreen got out of there as fast as she could. It wasn't very good if even the grocery store workers noted how little food Doreen was buying. But then what was she supposed to do? Money wasn't exactly growing on trees. And then she laughed because, of course, if someone had a quince tree and if someone could make jam, well, maybe money did grow on trees.

As soon as Doreen got home, she unpacked her groceries and then loaded up the animals in her car, not sure that she wanted to carry jam home on foot, and drove to the quince tree. Because she didn't know what the front of Esther's house looked like, Doreen walked up the alleyway once again and stood here, wondering if she should open the gate.

When the querulous voice on the other side said, "You might as well come in. Your animals are welcome in the yard too."

Doreen opened the gate and poked her head in. "I wasn't sure if you wanted me at the back here or in the front."

"Well, the back's fine if you'll eat quince right off the tree," she teased, "but they're not for everybody."

"Not sure I've ever had them like that," Doreen noted. Suddenly she was ushered inside Esther's backyard. As she stepped within the fencing, and her animals followed her— all on their best behavior this time—she noted not just quince, but apple trees and pear trees and what looked like brambleberries and raspberries. "Wow, you have a lot of fruits growing here."

"I do," she agreed, "and, for the decades that I could manage it, it was a godsend." Esther handed Doreen a basket. "I picked these all for you."

And, indeed, a lot of fruit was in this basket. "Oh, wow," Doreen said, "these are lovely."

"I'm hoping you'll eat them all," she stated, "unless you're watching your weight."

"I'm not watching my weight," she replied, "except watching it fall off me."

At that, the older lady burst into cackles. "Hey, lack of money can be the best weight loss program there is," she noted. "Now come on into the house. I put aside some jams for you."

And Doreen followed Esther up the decrepit stairs to a very old rickety house, glad to see Goliath and Mugs were happily lying amid the weeds back there, sniffing at the ground. "Your place reminds me of my grandmother's."

"You're living in your grandmother's place, aren't you?"

"Yes, I am," she said. "Nan's in Rosemoor."

"Ah, poor woman," she replied.

"I might have agreed with you on that, before I saw her there, but she's really happy."

At that, Esther turned and looked at her. "But do you think she's just trying to be happy for your sake?"

"No, I don't. I know she's happy there. She gets meals,

without having to cook them. She has friends. She has company when she wants. She has lawn bowling and movies and cards and all kinds of activities that keep her on her toes all the time," she shared. "I mean, sometimes I have to wait in line to see her because of her schedule."

"That wouldn't suit me at all," Esther declared. "I like my privacy."

"That's kind of the way I am too," Doreen admitted, "but Nan is happy."

"Good," Esther replied, "more power to her."

As they entered the house, heading to the front of it, the mustiness was getting to Doreen. "Smells like you've had a lot of water problems in here."

"I don't know if it's water problems or not," Esther noted, "but the house is old. It will go into the ground at the same time I do."

It was such a strange thing to say that Doreen looked at Esther in surprise.

The old lady cackled. "My son has been telling me for years that he'll drop it, and, if I don't die soon, he'll drop it whether I'm there or not."

"Oh my. I presume he's teasing you, right?"

"He will level the place, when the time comes. He says it would be easier that way, instead of trying to repair everything that's wrong with it. Plus, he thinks this place is a health hazard. Keeps threatening to do whatever he needs to do to get this place cleaned up. I told him to send them on. They can work and clean or whatever around me." Then she had a good chuckle.

Well, Doreen wouldn't argue with the son about this building being a health hazard because it was definitely a musty, moldy place. But then again, what did she know?

Maybe it was always that way.

And just then Esther claimed, "Honestly, it's always been this way. I'm just used to it. But for people coming inside for the first time, it can smell pretty rough."

Doreen didn't say anything because, well, what was there to say? The woman was right. It did smell pretty rough. At the kitchen, which was almost as ancient as Esther was, Doreen stopped to look around. "Kind of feels like my home," she noted quietly.

At that, the older woman looked at her. "Nan lived in her house for quite a while. I guess she didn't do much with it, did she?"

"No, she didn't," Doreen agreed. "She did there for a while, but it needs a fair bit of work."

"That's all right," Esther stated. "Take your time. You'll get there."

"Maybe," she replied. "Not the easiest thing to be working on all the time."

"No, it certainly isn't," she admitted. "I gave up on fixing a lot of this stuff. Now I just live here, accepting that there are limitations to the property. It's made me a lot happier."

And Doreen could completely understand that. As she stood here, the woman pointed to the table.

"So here are fifteen jars of my quince jam." She added, "Plus a couple jars of mincemeat, couple jars of pickles, and a dozen canned peaches." She turned to Doreen and frowned. "Wasn't sure how much you wanted."

"Well, I'm happy to have all of it," she stated honestly. "So how about I take what you're offering and thank you very much for it?"

The woman smiled. "It's nice to see somebody your age

not shying away from good home-canned stuff," she stated. "A lot of the younger generation are scared of it."

Doreen almost winced but managed to hold it back before the other woman saw it because, of course, that had been her own thoughts right from the beginning too. But, as she looked at the jars, everything was clean and sealed beautifully, so surely there couldn't be any reason not to have it. She looked over at Esther. "I really do appreciate this," she said sincerely.

The woman stared for a moment and then nodded. "You know what? I can see that. Anyway, here's a box, if you want to pack it up, so you only need one trip to take it out to your car."

"Thank you." She quickly put everything into the box. As soon as she had it all loaded, she picked up the box, hefted it, then nodded and smiled. "I can get this out to my car just fine." And she turned and headed toward the back door. At the door she stopped, turned to look at Esther. "I really do appreciate it, thank you."

"Call me Esther," she said. "It seems forever since I've used that name though."

"Why is that?"

"Aw, it's just I don't get very many visitors," she shared, her voice getting thick. "After my husband died, I just didn't want to see anybody else."

Doreen nodded. "I can understand that too."

"You married?"

"I was," she replied, "and now I can't seem to get rid of him."

And, for some reason, that made the other woman laugh uproariously. "Oh my goodness. That's too funny." As she waved her off, she added, "Go, have a good life."

"Do you want the jars back?" she asked automatically, knowing that was done within many of the communities.

The woman shook her head. "No, by the time you're finished eating all this, I'll be dead and gone anyway."

Doreen stopped at that comment. "Are you close to dying?"

"We're all close to dying," the older woman stated quietly. "You remember that. One day to the next could be your last."

And it was so true, and Doreen had seen it time and time again, so that she nodded in agreement. "No, I agree with you there. Life is precious. We should all be enjoying it." And, with that, she smiled and headed outside again.

When she reached the back gate, she found the older woman lumbering behind her slowly.

"I'm sorry," she apologized. "I should have gone out the front door. Then you wouldn't have to come back here."

"Doesn't matter," she replied. "I'll check the tree for that stupid magpie. Between him and the crows, they are robbing me daily."

"What do you mean?" Doreen asked.

"He took a safety pin off my deck here the other day," she noted, grumbling. "I needed it."

At that, Doreen frowned, then asked, "Do you have another one?"

"That's not the point," she snapped. "That magpie will steal anything."

Doreen hesitated and then realized that Esther's battle with the magpie was likely something ongoing for many years, and probably nothing Doreen could do would make it end right now.

She quickly walked out to the back gate, animals in tow,

smiled again, and said, "Thank you." Esther just nodded and waved. Even as Doreen unlocked her car, she heard the other woman pounding the tree with a stick.

"Aha, there you are, you little thief." And the caw of a magpie followed, obviously not impressed at being disturbed.

Doreen smiled at their antics and quickly loaded up her box of goodies and her animals and headed home.

Chapter 8

Back at home, Doreen quickly unloaded her treasure trove of treats from Esther. And after carrying them inside, she put on the teakettle and phoned Nan. "Hey, Nan. I just got quite a bunch of treats from Esther. She saw me in the grocery store and told me to come and get some."

At that, Nan squealed in delight. "Did you get jam?"

"Yeah, I did, and a bunch of other stuff. I just don't know …" She hesitated and then continued. "Well, I hate to say it, but I don't know if it's safe to eat."

"I'm coming," Nan replied. "Put on the teakettle, girl— and maybe toast, if you have it." And, with that, she hung up.

Surprised at the crazy reaction from Nan, Doreen knew that Nan probably wouldn't be long or far behind. By the time Doreen had put away her groceries and all but one of the three loaves of bread she'd bought, leaving it out for toast, she walked down to the creek with the animals to find Nan puffing along toward her. She waved enthusiastically.

"How on earth," Nan asked, as the two women met and greeted each other, "did you manage to get jam from Esther? She stopped selling it years ago."

"Well, I crossed paths with her at the grocery store, and she questioned me because I wasn't buying much," she noted. "She told me that I needed jam to go with peanut butter, and I said the budget didn't go that far, and I don't know for sure, but it's almost like she got offended."

At that, Nan nodded sagely. "Yep, that would offend her. She doesn't eat peanut butter and always was a champion for the fact that jam was the best thing on toast and biscuits."

"Well, I don't know how good her jam is," she replied, "but Esther told me to meet her at the house this afternoon, and, when I got there, she had all these jars set out for me." She pointed back at the house. "I'll show you when we get inside because I've got the table full."

When they walked into the kitchen, Nan started to ooh and aah immediately. "Wow, she must have really liked you."

"I don't think that was so much it," Doreen argued. "I just met her. I told you about the other day, when I was downtown, walking around?" She quickly improvised to avoid mentioning she was working on that diamond case. "Anyway, she called me out on my lack of jam in my grocery cart, so this is what she gave me today."

"Well, this is a horde," she noted enviously.

"You can take a jar back with you," Doreen offered generously. "I mean, if you love it that much, I certainly won't stop you from taking some."

Nan immediately reached out and snagged two.

Doreen burst out laughing. "Or you can take two."

Nan chuckled. "You haven't tasted this stuff," she exclaimed. "Something's magical about her quince trees. I don't know why, and nobody else ever seemed to really make jam like hers. The others were never quite the same. But I tell you, the fruit she gets from her trees, it's absolutely delicious."

"I'm looking forward to it."

"Do you have any bread?"

"Yep, I just bought three loaves."

At that, Nan raised an eyebrow and didn't say anything.

"You know some days are easier than others," Doreen explained to her grandmother.

"I do. Absolutely I do. We need to get you that money from those antiques."

"We do, indeed." Doreen sighed. "And I did ask Mack about Robin's estate because I may inherit something there but with probate?" She shrugged. "Who knows how long that will take?"

"Yep, could be next spring before you get that," Nan noted, "particularly as they can't sell the property until then."

"Really?" she asked.

"Any sale of property is done after probate's over. You can have the deal all set up and ready to go, but it can't be signed off on until the probate court closes its case."

"Oh." Doreen frowned. "Okay, I guess I'm not getting any money for a while then."

"Maybe not," Nan agreed, "and I don't know about Robin's probate case in particular, but, if you really need money, maybe you should talk to Nick about that legal stuff. Because, if you're the only beneficiary, surely he can speak to Robin's executor to give you something to tide you over."

"I don't know. Yet Mack suggested that same thing," she replied, "but I feel bad asking about it."

At that, Nan looked at her, with one eyebrow cocked,

like a Thaddeus gimlet glare. "Bad enough to starve?"

She winced. "Right, I need to think of it that way," she muttered.

Nan chuckled. "It really is simple when you consider things. You need money, even if it's a few thousand dollars, to help you out for a while."

"It would last me for many months, indeed," she declared, perking up. "Maybe I will say something to Nick."

"Do," Nan urged. "Just a simple question. It won't take that much to, you know, screw up your pride and simply ask. You've got it coming anyway."

"I'll call Nick later," Doreen stated, nodding, "after we have tea and jam."

"Now that's an idea." Nan rubbed her hands together. "You have no idea what kind of a treat we have in store for us now."

"I'm hoping I do," she replied, laughing. "I haven't had a good homemade jam in a very long time."

"Well, let's get some of that toast on then."

By the time the toaster buzzed, they had tea steeping, and Nan had already opened the first jar. Immediately she dipped in her spoon and had a taste right off the spoon. She closed her eyes and gave a happy sigh. "You have no idea what a treasure you have here," she murmured.

Staring at Nan and the look of rapture on her face, Doreen noted, "Nan, you realize it's just jam, right?"

Nan immediately opened her eyes and narrowed them at her.

"Okay," Doreen backtracked quickly, "so apparently this jam is something special. I thought I'd tried it before but now I'm not so sure."

"Try it," Nan said. "And then mock me at your own

peril."

But rather than having her first taste of Esther's stupendous jam on a spoon, like her nan had done, Doreen buttered a piece of toast and then added some quince jam. As she bit into it, the special flavor filled her mouth. She stared at Nan in surprise.

Nan was cackling again. "See? See?" Nan asked.

Doreen snatched two pieces of toast, quickly buttered them, and then slathered them with jam. She sat down with an expression of sheer delight on her face.

"This? You have no idea how I miss this." Nan eyed the jars with envy and stated, "I'll buy some off you."

She stared at her grandmother. "Nan, you can just have some."

"Nope, nope, nope, nope." Nan shook her head heartily. "A haul like this deserves to be paid for."

"I don't feel very good about selling you anything," she explained. "You're my grandmother, for heaven's sake. If you would like some, take some."

"Oh no," she repeated.

"And what happens if it gets back to Esther that I sold her jam that she generously gave to me for free?" Doreen asked. "That would make me feel even worse."

At that, Nan frowned. "Fine," she grumbled. "I won't necessarily buy it from you. I'll leave you a donation. And I'll take three more."

By the time Nan was ready to go, she had six jam jars in her little stash.

Doreen stared at it and asked, "You think you have enough now?"

Nan gave her another gimlet look. "For now."

"And you won't sell it, will you?" Doreen warned. "Because I don't want you taking it back to Rosemoor and selling it to anybody there."

"No, absolutely not," she declared, with a huff. "Nobody'll know about it because, if they found out about it, they'll be trying to steal it from me. No, no, no," Nan stated once more. "And this way, you'll be totally covered, and Esther won't even know."

"If I give you a jar, and she does find out, she won't take it so badly. Surely I'm allowed to give my grandmother a jar. Especially as I did tell Esther that you really loved it."

"I used to buy it from her all the time. Broke my heart when she wouldn't sell me any more."

"It sounds like she needed it for herself."

"Yep, she did," Nan agreed. "Yet, at the same time, she was being stubborn because she wouldn't let anybody help her in her jam production." But then Nan shrugged. "Then I could say that about a lot of people." And she shot Doreen a hard look.

Doreen flushed. "You've helped me so much, Nan."

And Nan immediately nodded. "Yep, and I'll help you some more. But first, let's enjoy all of our blessings right now."

And she put on two more pieces of bread in the toaster. As soon as the toast was done, they sat outside on the deck and slowly ate toast and jam. Done with her first two pieces, Doreen sat beside her nan and just had a cup of tea, as she watched her grandmother enjoy four pieces of toast, topped by Esther's jam.

"Glad I could do something for you today," Doreen admitted, with a gentle smile.

Nan looked over at her, wrapped her arms around her granddaughter, and gave her a gentle hug. "Just being here does a lot for me. Don't ever forget that."

Chapter 9

Wednesday Morning

DOREEN WOKE THE next morning, still amused at Nan's reaction to the jam. Jelly actually—at least she thought it was more jelly than jam. She had to admit that Nan was right; Esther's jelly was absolutely delicious. But Doreen didn't have much of a sweet tooth herself and preferred peanut butter over jam on her toast. The two together, of course, were nirvana, but, when one had to make a financial choice, Doreen opted for the one that would feed her body, not just her soul.

With a smile, she checked on her animals, two in bed with her. Thaddeus was on his roost. Doreen shook her head. They were support animals in many ways for her. Goliath, despite his diffident attitude, loved her, and not just because she fed him. At that thought, the Maine coon patted his furry chubby paw to her lips. "I love you too, Goliath."

At her words, Mugs woofed and walked all over her to give her a sloppy kiss on her face. Not to be ignored, Thaddeus spoke. "Thaddeus loves Doreen. Thaddeus loves Doreen." Doreen had to laugh. She did, indeed, feel well loved in Kelowna, surrounded by these three and her grandmother. They all had saved her and had shown her a better life here.

And now there was Mack too.

She got up and had a quick shower, headed downstairs, seeing the almost empty jelly jar still sitting on the counter, and chuckled. She quickly sent Nan a text. **Did you have jam this morning?**

She got an instant response. **Of course.**

Doreen smiled at that. After she put on her coffee, she fed her trio, then looked at the kitchen table, still covered by Esther's gifts. Doreen picked up one of the sealed jars, took another look at it, and decided to find someplace to put them—maybe where Nan didn't necessarily see them all the time. Doreen was more than happy to share and to give her grandmother as much as she wanted, but Nan obviously had a slight addiction problem with Esther's jellies.

On that thought, Doreen went to the pantry and found a mostly empty cupboard and started putting away the jars. When she picked up the last couple jars, she found something tucked underneath. As she pulled out the money, she gasped. Once again Nan was up to her usual tricks. Doreen hadn't wanted Nan to pay for the jam.

Doreen stared at the cash, and her heart clenched, knowing how much her grandmother cared and how often she found excuses to put money into Doreen's hands. Doreen immediately picked up the phone and called her. When her grandmother answered, she was chuckling to somebody in the same room.

"Nan, you didn't have to," Doreen said, trying hard to contain the emotions in her voice.

At that, Nan stopped, realized what she was talking about, and whispered, "I never *have* to. It is my joy to. And, if you feel like coming down and having tea with me today, I'd love to see you. Right now I'm heading out to lawn bowling. So I love you, and I'm leaving now." And, with that, she hung up.

Doreen stared down at the phone and started to chuckle. That was Nan all over. And, if Doreen understood one thing, it was how blessed she was to have Nan in her life. She quickly put away the $200.00. Adding this to Wendy's money—provided the check cleared Doreen's account—was a godsend and would get her through all of this month and more.

And, with that, she sat down at her laptop, with her second cup of coffee, logged in to ensure the check had cleared, and then paid the bills she owed. With that done, she still had money enough for a good-size grocery shopping trip and a tank of gas.

So, on the same roll, she got up, grabbed a notepad, and made a grocery list, putting the animals' food at the top, so that she could get them several more months' worth stocked ahead, and she wouldn't have to worry about that for a while. She knew she could always borrow money from Nan if needed, but that wasn't the same thing as being independent on her own.

Sure, it was a bit of a joke to think that Doreen was being independent, when Nan kept doing things like this, but they were gifts that came from the heart, and Doreen wouldn't stop her grandmother from doing something that brought her obvious joy either. Doreen shook her head.

After living the rich lifestyle before, and not even really realizing it from a practical pay-the-bills standpoint, now that she was on the poorer end of life, she vowed she would never take money for granted. She was learning to be a good steward with what money she had, and she felt very proud of that. And she was happy to have someone to help her, when needed. What did people, like Esther, who had no one to rely on, do?

With Esther's goodies behind a closed door now, Doreen double-checked her grocery list, looked to the animals, and shared, "Now I can go shopping, or we can go out into the garden and do some work there."

Her animals didn't respond. Mugs rolled over, as if completely uninterested in the choices.

"I'm not sure what else to do," she bemoaned. "We don't have a whole lot to go on with our case for Wendy."

But then, thinking about it, Doreen wondered. She picked up her phone yet again and phoned Wendy. "Hey. It's Doreen. I just want to know if you've had any more visitors."

"No." And, although relief was evident in her voice, worry was also present that they would return at any time.

"Do you often have a group of magpies around or a murder of crows in the alley around the dumpsters?"

"Lots of them," she noted. "A woman on this lane has fruit trees, and that brings birds from all over the place. Plus, we businesspeople all put out our commercial garbage there, in all those bins up and down the back alleyway. So, yeah, of course we have lots of birds and rodents and bugs and things. Yet I've never had any problems with them. Why do you ask?"

"I just wondered," Doreen replied thoughtfully.

"Well, if you're wondering something," Wendy mentioned, with a laugh, "maybe keep me in the loop, so I'm not broadsided by any questions Mack might throw at me."

"Hopefully he won't be throwing any that you can't

handle," she noted. "Has he contacted you?"

"He did, yes, when he stopped in the shop. We had a bit of a discussion about what had gone on. He took a look around, kind of nodded, and told me that, rather than phoning you when I get into trouble, I should be phoning the police." Then she laughed. "It's almost like he knew."

"Oh, he does know," Doreen agreed, with a sigh. "And now part of his job is keeping me out of his world."

"And keeping you safe," Wendy added, with almost noticeable envy in her voice. "You may not realize it, but you're very lucky."

Doreen thought about that statement long after she'd hung up. She wasn't sure how—from one day to the next—she'd ended up with both Nan and Mack, but, in both cases, she had been extremely lucky. Granted, Nan was family, and Doreen didn't choose her. Yet, if it had been left to Doreen, she would have chosen Nan to be her grandmother anyway.

As for Mack? She had been putting him off, and now she realized how risky that was. He could have thought her too much effort or too damaged to continue his pursuit of her. Luckily she wised up enough to choose him, before he chose someone else.

Doreen was lucky to have people who cared about her and people she cared about. Deciding that maybe a day at home would be just the thing she needed, she got out her gardening gloves after breakfast. She figured to get some work done in her backyard garden, before any of the summer afternoon heat hit, and then she could do a bit of shopping later. With a wheelbarrow at hand, she quickly started pulling out the weeds and cleaning up along the garden edges.

Having so much free landscaping work done back here,

with the installations of all the walkways and the deck and the patio, now made her job so much easier. She had clean-cut divides between walkways and the lawn or the gardens. It made even her workload look better because she could see what remained to be done—instead of being overwhelmed by the amount of unending work. She whistled to herself, so happy to be outside and to be working in her own garden, with her animals all around her as she weeded, when her phone rang.

She answered it without thinking, saying, "Hello," in a bright cheerful tone. When silence came on the other end, she frowned and looked down at it and winced. "Hello?" she said a second time.

"Why are you so damn happy?" her soon-to-be-ex-husband snapped.

She sighed. "I'm not supposed to talk to you."

"Oh, you're *not supposed to be talking to me*," he mocked, "but you are too late."

She glared down at the phone. "And I *really* won't talk to you if you make fun of me like that." She quickly hung up. Knowing that she'd be in trouble if she didn't say anything, she immediately contacted Mack's brother, Nick.

He answered the phone by saying, "Just the woman I want to talk to."

"Maybe not," she stated, with a sigh. "My ex just called me."

Nick was immediately all business. "What did he want?"

"I don't know, but he started to mock me, so I hung up on him."

After a moment of silence, he chuckled. "You know what? I really like that."

"I figured you would get upset if you found out I was

talking to him."

"Yeah, I sure would," he stated quietly. "He should not have called you in the first place. Everything is to go through the attorneys of the two parties to the divorce."

"Well, I don't even know what he wanted, but he ruined my good mood." She raised her free hand. "He immediately got angry at me and asked why I was in such a good mood."

"Ah, so sour grapes on his part."

"I'm not sure what the sour grapes are," she noted, "but he's not in a good mood. However, that is not so different for him. I'm really hoping that you can tell me that he's not anywhere close by."

At that, Nick asked, "Are you afraid he is?"

"I don't know about *afraid*," she replied cautiously. "Given the surliness of his tone, I wouldn't want him to pop by suddenly."

"As far as I know, he's still in Vancouver," he noted quietly. "However, if he does show up …"

"Don't worry. I'll be calling Mack," she stated.

"Glad to hear it."

"Did you get anywhere on the divorce agreement?" she asked curiously. "Is that why he's in such a pissy mood?"

"Oh, that's part of it. Also the fact that I'm more than willing to go to court over this one," he explained. "And he doesn't want to go before a judge."

"Why not?" she asked in a reasonable tone. "Isn't that one way to handle it?"

"Definitely it's one way to handle it, but it's one way that he'll lose."

"Ah, meaning that he's in the wrong, and you think the judge will favor my side of this."

"It's not even so much that the judge will favor you as

he'll favor the law. And, in this case, you get the benefit. After all, you were married for fourteen years and helped grow his business. And, of course, your husband seems to think that you shouldn't get anything."

"That's pretty typical of him," she noted. When Nick remained silent, she added, "So let me ask you a question. If you were handling somebody's estate, and one person is due to get something out of the estate, but it hasn't finished the probate process. What if they contact you and ask about getting a little bit of money ahead of time?"

"Ah, you're talking about Robin's will?"

"Yeah. ... Don't get me wrong. I'm okay for the month."

"But you're only okay. And only for one month?"

"Well, I'm a whole lot better today than I was yesterday, and yesterday I was a whole lot better than I was the day before. So honestly, I'm probably not in a position to ask for that yet," she shared. "I just wondered, if things got really ugly, is that something I could do?"

"You can always ask. Robin's executor could contact the probate lawyer to see how much money is there and available."

"But there's property to be sold," she added.

"Right. But she had money to live off of, like in bank accounts and cash and the like. So, unless her financial accounts are 100 percent empty, some available money should be there."

"Maybe, I don't know anything about her assets."

"It's certainly something that's been asked before of the attorneys and the estate and even the court. I guess it would be up to the probate lawyer as to whether he wanted to be nice enough and help you out. And whether he felt that enough money was there to cover your request."

"Right. I was hoping for maybe even one thousand dollars. That would cover my bills for several months."

"Is that all you need?" he asked in surprise.

"I'm sure you've heard about all the antiques and stuff," she explained. "There should be some of that auction money coming to me. I just don't know how long that takes. Like I think money is supposedly coming from Robin's will, but I'm not sure how much longer I need to wait."

"Right. So you have money out there that is due you. However, it's just not here yet."

"Exactly, so I'm struggling to get through to those payouts." And then she hesitated. "Never mind. Forget I even asked."

"You know what? If it's that bad," he noted, "definitely try asking."

"Well, if I get that bad, I will," she replied. "I'm checking out my options before I get there."

"Probate can be slow, especially if you're really needy," he added. "And I'm not privy to Robin's estate case, so I'm not aware of any other liens or court cases or anything related to Robin's estate that must be paid for first. If so, the probate lawyer will withhold funds to pay any of those debts. Therefore, that process may take a while. However, with the antiques auction, you should get some settlement within a few months."

"So not so soon with the probate? Maybe more like one year?"

"Yes, that's true." He hemmed and hawed. "Look. If you ever need a thousand dollar loan, you can always let me know."

"Nope, nope, nope, nope," she cried out. "Thank you

very much for the offer, but I think Mack would kill me."

Nick burst out laughing. "So now you're afraid of Mack?"

"No, I'm not afraid of Mack, but I wouldn't want to insult him."

"And you think asking me for money or me helping you with money would be an insult?"

"Yes, because he would say that I should have gone to him first."

At that, there was silence first. "Oh, I do like you. And you know what? If you ever want to get rid of that brother of mine, you could always give me a call." And, with that, he hung up on her.

She stared down at the phone. "It must be catching," she muttered. "Nobody would ever have hung up on me before. But now it seems like everybody does."

She rolled her eyes at that and continued with her gardening. But she had to admit she felt this weird sense of always looking over her shoulder now. As if afraid that her dear ex was on his way to her. And that would be very disturbing. And yet it would be something he would do, phoning first to confirm that she was home and then getting pissed off because she sounded so happy at life, even though he could, in theory, have called her from just around the corner.

On that thought, she bolted to her feet and searched for Mugs, Thaddeus, and Goliath. "Let's go inside."

And she quickly packed up her gardening stuff, and they all headed inside. On sheer instincts alone, Doreen locked up and set the alarm. Even then, she sat in the living room with a cup of tea and just waited, hating that sensation of something bad about to happen. She didn't know what was coming or where it was coming from, but that phone call from her ex had set her off. And, even now, she couldn't find any way to make things feel better.

When her phone rang a little later, she sighed with relief when Mack's name popped up on her phone's Caller ID and so answered his call. "Hey," she answered, trying for some neutral tone.

"What's wrong?" he asked immediately.

She sighed. "How come you know something's wrong?" she muttered. "Here I was trying so hard to act normal."

"Well, acting normal for you just means you sound very unnatural."

"*Great*," she muttered to herself. "Good thing I'm not trying for a career in the arts."

He chuckled. "Now that you feel better, tell me what's going on."

"Oh, I spoke with your brother earlier," she replied. "And unfortunately—although everything's fine with him, and everything is on target—I also got a phone call from my ex."

"What did he want?" Mack asked in ominous tones.

"I'm not really sure. He didn't really say anything. He just got mad because I had been in a very good mood," she explained, "and then he seemed to get really ugly. So I hung up on him. I didn't even give him a chance to talk, but, of course, I immediately felt guilty."

"Of course you hung up on the jerk because my brother told you not to talk to him."

"Sure, but I answered the phone without checking the Caller ID. I was outside, gardening. I wasn't thinking. I had just hit Talk and said hello."

"And you didn't recognize his number?"

She thought about it. "No, I didn't," she replied in surprise. "I wonder if it's a different one."

"Maybe. So now what's the matter? Did he upset you?"

"No, he didn't really upset me. He took away my good mood, just hearing his voice," she noted. "But then I was also a little worried after the conversation with your brother. And, no, Nick didn't say anything to upset me. No, there's nothing that I should tell you about or anything else," she explained. "I just got that weird feeling, while I was in the backyard, and I came racing inside and locked all the doors."

There was a moment of silence on the other end. "Are you afraid Mathew is in town? Did he say anything about seeing you?"

"Well, I'm definitely afraid of something. I'm not totally sure what that's all about—feeling pretty foolish actually." And then she gave a nervous laugh. "I don't know where it's coming from honestly."

"You mean, after the number of times you've been attacked, where you've turned around in your house to find a stranger there, or the number of times that people who supposedly were your friends really haven't been your friends? Gee, I don't think you have to go looking for a reason as to why you could be having an attack of nerves. And, as far as I have ever seen, your husband, ... ex-husband, has never done that to you, but given the circumstances ..."

"I know," she agreed. "I also asked your brother about whether the probate lawyer might let me have some money out of Robin's estate early. Nick mentioned it could very well just be up to the person's own discretion."

"And I guess that makes sense. The probate attorney has the responsibility of paying the rightful people any money Robin owed them. Whatever's left over would be yours, if she designated it all to you. Yeah, he wouldn't give you too much to get through in the meantime though."

"Then I would only need a thousand dollars or maybe a couple to make it through the next few months," she noted, "at least until the antiques come through."

"And you got the catalog for the antiques auction, so how does everything look?" he asked.

She realized he was trying to bolster her mood and to change the conversation just enough to make her feel better, and she appreciated it, but, at the same time, she wasn't terribly sure she wanted to feel better necessarily. "I think it looks great," she replied, looking around for it. "And I've misplaced the darn thing right now."

"I suggest you find it, sit down, take a moment, enjoy knowing that you'll get money coming after the auction," he noted quietly. "Of course remember that some things might sell, and some things might not. You just need to hold on a little bit longer." He hesitated. "Did my brother say anything else?"

"Yes." She laughed. "He told me that, if I got in trouble, he would be more than happy to give me a loan."

"He said that?" Mack asked. "I have never known my brother to ever offer anybody money."

"I turned him down nicely."

"And why would you do that?" he asked curiously. "It's obvious you could use a few bucks."

"Yep, but I also told him that you would be furious if I did that."

At that came more silence. "You know that I would never be furious at you for something like that," he stated cautiously.

"Yeah, you would," she argued, "because, as far as you're

concerned, I should have asked you first."

After another long moment came his reply, and more than just the words but the way he delivered them were like a hug that she desperately needed.

"And *that* I would consider major progress in our relationship. Now you stay inside, comfy and warm," he said, "and I'll stop by later today. If you see your ex, don't answer the door, just call me immediately. I have to go." And, with that, he rang off.

She smiled, as she put down her phone. "At least I did something right," she muttered.

Chapter 10

EXCEPT THAT DOREEN didn't want to sit inside for the rest of the afternoon and do nothing. Although she did have all those notes on Bernard and Candy from her latest trip to the library that she hadn't had a chance to go through yet either. So, considering that, she grabbed her tea, took that and her laptop with her notes, and headed over to the living room, where she sat down and went through everything that she had found on the yellow diamond ring. It was huge; there was no price tag to put on it.

She didn't know what the largest yellow diamond in the world was worth, but she imagined it was a pretty big figure, with a lot of zeros involved in any kind of purchase price. But, as she'd come to learn, people would kill over the slightest thing, so whether it was worth millions or multiple millions really didn't matter. It was something that was worthwhile for any criminal element to go after—if they knew who had it or what had happened to it. But then, if somebody knew what happened to it, blackmail might be an easier target as well. She pondered that for a moment.

That Wendy had no security images of the woman who'd tried to sell the ring to Wendy was frustrating.

Doreen pondered the whole event.

"No, no, that makes no sense," she argued out loud. "Anybody with half a brain would have taken it to a jeweler or a pawnshop. No way they would have gone to a little side-street consignment store. So what was going on with that? Unless they thought for sure the ring they had was costume jewelry. But, if it were costume jewelry, why the $10,000 selling price? And why the disguise? Costume jewelry would have gotten the woman maybe ten bucks."

No, as Doreen thought about it, probably wouldn't even have gotten her that much. Wendy might have maybe sold it for ten bucks, if it were a special piece, but costume jewelry was cheap, cheap, cheap. Nobody put out big money on it. So none of this made any sense.

As she sat here, continuing to think about it, she picked up the phone and contacted Wendy.

When Wendy heard Doreen's voice, she whispered, "They're here. Oh my God, they're here."

"Okay," she stated. "Did you phone Mack?"

"No, I can't. I can't." And she hung up on Doreen.

Doreen immediately phoned Mack, and, when she couldn't get him directly, she left a message, and then sat here, wondering what she should do. Didn't take her long to decide, and she bolted to her feet, grabbed the animals, loaded everybody in the car, and raced down to Wendy's shop.

As soon as she got there, she entered the store with a bright smile on her face to find Wendy standing frozen at the cash register, trying to look natural.

When she caught Doreen's gaze, Wendy rolled her eyes toward the back door. Immediately Doreen walked to the back with the animals, stepped outside into the alleyway and saw the men. "Hey. You guys again. What are you up to?" And she acted so normal and natural that they just stared at her.

"We want to see Wendy."

"Wendy's busy dealing with the customers in the store right now," she replied, "which I'm sure you already know."

"I don't care," the lead guy of the two stated in an odd voice. "And we don't give a crap who you are. Go get Wendy."

"I won't go get Wendy. She's dealing with a paying customer," Doreen replied. "So what is your problem?"

"None of your business."

"Unless, of course, you're coming after that ring."

At that, both men pinned her in place with their glares. "What do you know about a ring?"

"Only what Wendy told me about some crazy lady coming in, all dolled up with a disguise, trying to sell a ring."

"She shouldn't be trying to sell no rings here," the man stated, looking around the corner of the alleyway.

"Right. That's what Wendy told the woman. I mean, Wendy sells secondhand clothing. It's hardly a pawnshop."

"What do you know about pawnshops?" he asked.

"I don't know anything about them," she replied cheerfully. "Friend of mine does though."

"And who's that?" he asked, with a sneer.

"His name's Mack. You probably don't know him." And then she looked at him, snickered, and added, "Well, maybe you do."

At that, he stared at her. "What do you mean?"

She laughed. "I mean, it depends if you have a record or not. Mack's a cop. Good friend of mine."

"Yeah right, lady." He shook his head. "You think we

haven't heard crap like that before?"

"Oh, I'm sure you have," she agreed, "but Mack really is a cop."

"*Right.*" He rolled his eyes. "Threats like that won't get you anywhere."

"Threats?" she repeated in astonishment in a completely innocent tone of voice. "Good Lord, why would I want to threaten you? You're way bigger than I am." She shrugged. "But I really can't have you being mean to poor Wendy."

He huffed and shook his head. "Then get us the ring," he demanded in a threatening manner.

"*Get you the ring?* Ha, pretty sure you didn't hear me when I said that Wendy told her no."

"No way Wendy would have told her no," he argued. "Anybody could have seen what a ring it was."

"If that woman had sold it to Wendy, then it would be Wendy's, wouldn't it?"

"Except that it was stolen," the other guy stated less pleasantly. "And we want it back."

"Oh, so it's yours, is it?" she asked, smirking.

He just stared at her, with that look that said that she was really starting to piss him off.

"You know I've seen that look a time or two," she noted. "You really don't have much patience, do you?" The man's glare deepened. She nodded. "I guess not." She looked down at Mugs. "He really doesn't like us, buddy."

Mugs barked in response.

She laughed. "Yeah, I know. We get that a lot."

"Yeah, ya think? You're really starting to piss me off. Now," he said, talking louder, "we want the ring."

"That's nice, but we don't have the ring," she stated gently. "Do you really think Wendy would still be here if she'd bought some fancy ring that was obviously worth way more than she'd supposedly paid for it?"

He stared at her, frowning.

She shook her head. "Wendy is eking out a living selling secondhand clothing," she explained. "There's no money to be found in her industry. There's no money to be found in this store at all. It's foolish to even consider that she could even afford to buy the ring."

"Then she sold it," he stated, "and we want to know who bought it."

"And again, how could she afford to buy it in the first place? In the second place, how would she have known where to sell it?" she asked. "If it was something valuable, it's hardly something you can just turn around and sell any old place. Plus, you say it was stolen. Who would buy a stolen piece of jewelry, no matter how much you think it is worth? I don't know when it might have been stolen," she said, her gaze going from one man to the other, but neither of the men were budging. "And it's obvious that you're not talking, so ..." She shrugged. "Besides, if it was stolen, how do we know that it's even yours?"

"It's ours."

"Yeah? And who is this woman to you?" she asked, with a scoff. "Your mother?"

At that, he stiffened. And she wondered.

"Unless, of course, it *is* your mother," she suggested. "Or a sister maybe, somebody who was trying to sell a family heirloom to get back at you for something?" Then she added, "But that doesn't make sense because, if you had an expensive ring like that, you wouldn't hold on to it. Not you guys. You two are intent on exchanging it for cash, right?" Doreen frowned. "Surely if you had that ring for one second, then you would have sold it. I mean, if it's worth a lot of money—like you think it is—you guys would have already cashed it in."

"Well, aren't you just so smart," the leader replied in a dark tone. "Maybe you're a little too smart."

"Yeah, I've heard that a time or two." She studied the two men and then shrugged. "Okay, you don't want to talk, and I've already told you that we didn't have anything to do with it, so not sure where you could go from here," she muttered. "Unless you know who that lady was."

The leader just stared at her.

Seems like he has an idea about who she was. "I mean, you could check pawnshops. That lady would have been much better off to have gone there in the first place." She shrugged. "Well, of course, she would have. Like I said, something was very odd about her coming here in the first place. Wendy doesn't buy good quality jewelry. And she thought back then it was just a cheap costume piece of jewelry, but now you're making us rethink that."

"Obviously it wasn't a cheap piece," the leader stated, taking two steps toward her. "And you need to learn to shut your mouth."

She smiled at him, as Mugs resorted to growling. "You're not the first person to tell me that."

"I can imagine," he muttered. "Do you ever shut up?"

She thought about it and then shrugged. "Every once in a while I do, but, when you're here, threatening a friend of mine, that won't really go over so well, with me or my dog."

Mugs growled again, this time louder.

"I'll do more than threaten her if you don't come up with that ring," he stated, turning and walking back to his van. "You got two days."

"And then what?" she asked. "Because we don't have it, and we can tell you that right now."

"Then you better get it," he snapped. "Two days and we'll be back. If you don't have it, there won't be a lot left of the store or … Wendy."

Chapter 11

CHECKING HER PHONE to make sure the photo of the big white van had come out clear enough, Doreen stepped back into the store to find Wendy staring at her in horror.

"Did they just say what I think they did?" she squeaked.

"Yep, they sure did," Doreen confirmed in a dark tone. "They're pretty serious about this ring."

"I don't have it." Wendy raised both hands in frustration. "I didn't have anything to do with it."

"And that's what we'll have to get Mack to help us sort out," she muttered.

"Yeah, I hear you," Mack stated from the front entrance to Wendy's shop. "I got your message, but it was a bit garbled."

She motioned at Wendy. "Wendy can tell you what just happened."

Wendy, with a bit of encouragement, managed to get out the tale.

And then Doreen picked it up. "And I got this photo of the van." She showed it to Mack. "I can give you a basic description but not a whole lot. Both of the men looked quite comfortable uttering threats though."

"Of course they did," he noted, with a sigh. "And you got them quite angry, didn't you?"

"They needed to know that Wendy didn't have the ring," she stated.

He turned and looked at Wendy. "Do you have the ring?"

Surprised to hear Mack's question, Doreen turned and looked at Wendy.

But Wendy was shaking her head. "No, no, I don't. Something was very odd about the woman and everything to do with that ring. I mean, I don't know fine jewelry, but I presumed it wasn't costume, and I'm not a pawnshop, so I don't have the right clientele to offload something like that. Plus the woman wanted ten grand. *Cash*."

"From you?" Mack asked, then winced and shrugged, trying to smooth over his tone.

"Yes. I mean, do I look like I have ten thousand dollars lying around?" she asked, throwing her arms out wide. "I don't even take in that much in one month."

At that, Mack nodded slowly. "So what would be the purpose of that woman coming here to you?"

"A few things," Doreen replied quietly. "I've been thinking about this. One, she herself needs some professional assistance and doesn't really understand the facts of life and maybe doesn't really understand how pawnshops or anything like that works, so, in theory, she's just unstable mentally," she began. "Two, it was a cry for help, and she didn't know what else to do. Three, she just darted in here, maybe trying to escape somebody who was following her, or she purposely was trying to lead somebody here."

At that last one, Mack raised his eyebrows in consideration and turned and looked at Wendy. "So is there any reason why somebody would want to lead these goons to you?"

Wendy paled and shook her head. "I don't know why—out of all the things that she just suggested—you would jump onto that one."

"Because, out of all the things that she just offered, this is the only one that really makes any sense."

"No, bringing somebody to me doesn't make any sense," Wendy argued. "Obviously ten grand is something I didn't have, couldn't afford to exchange for some ring I might never sell, and wouldn't have given her that cash for a ring I couldn't get appraised, and I don't know enough about high-end jewelry to even know what I would do with it afterward."

"Right." He nodded. "So, what other purpose would anybody have for coming in here and doing that?"

"Did the woman sound desperate?" Doreen asked Wendy.

"Desperate, yes, but she was fairly calm. She did want ten thousand dollars. I told her that I didn't have it. And I couldn't give it to her even if I wanted to because I just didn't have that kind of money," she explained quietly. "Was she in trouble? I don't know." She showed her palms. "I don't deal with people like that. That's you guys' corner." She looked from one to the other.

"Well, it's Mack's domain," Doreen replied automatically.

He sighed. "It's not something that we supposedly deal with," he noted quietly. "Unfortunately, in cases where desperate people will do desperate things, it makes no sense to come here with an expensive and very unique ring like that and try to sell it. The fact of the matter is, you didn't give her the money, she left, and yet these guys seem to think that either you did give her the money or she has left the ring behind."

"The woman did mention that. She suggested that she could leave the ring behind and that she could come back later, once I had it appraised," Wendy admitted. "And I did think about it, but I don't know anything about jewelry. I don't know how much the appraisal would have cost. Even if I could have gotten the appraisal done instantly and paid for that, her purchase price of ten grand was still way more money than I had."

"Did she say anything else?" Mack asked suddenly. "Like, that you might have some connection to somebody you could talk to."

She stared at him. "No. I don't know anybody in the diamond trade. I mean, first off, I couldn't confirm it was a real diamond. Plus, she wasn't making a whole lot of sense, and, once I took a closer look at the ring and heard her selling price, no way I wanted any part of her and her ring. That was way more money than I could even contemplate handing over to anybody, and no way I wanted to get involved in a questionable transaction."

"And that probably surprised her," Mack noted, "because a lot of people wouldn't have questioned it or would quite likely have jumped at the opportunity."

"Maybe some diamond merchant, yeah. The whole conversation gave me the heebie-jeebies," she stated. "It was just such a huge stone that it seemed fake."

He nodded, pulled up his phone, flicked through several screenloads, and then held up his phone. "Did it look something like that?"

Wendy took the phone from him, staring at the picture for a long moment. "I'd say it looked exactly like that." She returned his phone to him and asked, "What is that ring?"

At that, Doreen held out her hand to look at it, and, when Mack hesitated, she glared at him, and he pulled the phone forward and held up the picture to her. Her eyebrows shot up. "Per my library research, that ring was stolen ten years ago," she said, looking at Wendy. "It was the engagement ring between Bernard and Candy."

"Bernard and Candy?" Wendy repeated, with a frown. And then her face cleared. "Oh my. Seriously?" She looked at the picture again. "Honestly it looked just like that picture. But I can't confirm that it was *that one* because I don't know anything about jewelry."

"Got it," Mack noted. "So now we have a problem. Not only do these thugs seem to think that you *should* know something about this, but, if they're looking for a ring like this, and they think it's here or that you have some knowledge of it, they won't walk away."

Wendy looked at him nervously, her hands wringing in front of her. "I guess it's worth a lot of money, isn't it?"

"It's worth millions," he replied quietly. "And that is now a whole different story."

After that, things happened a little faster. Mack put in a full report. Somebody else came to get descriptions and statements from them, as Mack looked over at Doreen. "And, of course, you're in the middle of this again."

She shrugged. "Technically it's a cold case." He glared at her. She just beamed.

"Can you describe the men?"

She frowned. "I thought I could, but now it feels very much like they were nondescript. Although I would recognize them again. They're definitely criminals and probably have long records, but I can't prove that."

"No, of course not." Mack groaned. "And that doesn't mean that they're from around here either."

"So, in other words, they could be imported." She nodded agreeably. He just rolled his eyes at that. "What? It makes sense. I mean, something like this diamond, they'll sell quickly. Once they have it. The question is, how did they get ahold of the diamond to begin with? Were these two goons the original thieves? I hardly think so. These two are the brawn, not the brains. So who did that woman steal the ring from? Who's been hanging on to the ring all this time? And why do these two thugs think it's theirs?"

"Well, that's the criminal mind-set for you. They think it's theirs," Mack stated in exasperation, "because they obviously heard about it, found out about it, or assumed that they were in the process of getting it. To them it's a done deal. It's all about money grabs."

She laughed. "Life's not quite like that."

"No. So this woman is either close to them or found out what they were doing and set off to do something completely off target that they don't understand either." Mack shook his head, considering the angles.

"And, of course, anybody like these goons would have just taken the ring and run," Doreen shared out loud. "Kinda like that strange woman did."

"Exactly." Mack glanced at Wendy, then turned to Doreen, lowered his voice, and asked, "And are you sure an exchange didn't happen?"

Doreen's gaze widened, as she understood what he was asking. She frowned, as she looked back at Wendy, who was busy talking to a police officer. "No, I can't guarantee it didn't happen," she replied quietly. "I would never have thought that of her. However," she paused, "maybe that woman left the diamond in a pocket to one of these outfits in here?"

He just continued to stare at her in that strong, steady way of his, and she sighed.

"So, of course, that could mean maybe the woman was working with Wendy? But the same argument applies. If Wendy has it, why would she be here? She could have taken that ring and run."

"That would have made her look suspicious. Also running still takes planning."

"But she didn't have to report it to anybody," Doreen noted quietly. "I mean, that stranger was obviously—" And then she stopped. "Unless she knew Wendy. And thought that this would trigger something for her."

"What do you mean?" Mack asked in interest.

"That can't be right," Doreen said, mostly to herself, shaking her head. "That would mean the two women knew each other, as in ten years ago when the theft happened. Like they were partners back then." Doreen shook her head more adamantly now. "No. I mean, it doesn't make sense that this strange woman would have come here. Wendy's shop is a secondhand store, not a jewelry store or a pawnshop."

Wendy heard her and turned and looked at her. "Exactly. It's not like I'm a bank—or a pawnshop or a jeweler—with cash on hand all the time. All I ever really wanted was to have my own business, be my own boss, and this seemed like a viable way to do it. But I don't harbor any illusions that I'll ever make a fortune at it."

The trouble was, her words didn't make Doreen feel any better. She nodded slowly and looked at Mack and then asked in a low voice, "Can I go home now?"

He sighed. "Have you given your statement?"

She rolled her eyes and nodded.

"I'm thinking about having you come down and look at mug shots."

"I can do that," she agreed immediately, interest in her voice.

"The guys at the station would not particularly like it," he noted, with a sigh, "but it might be a good step right now."

"If I recognize one of these men," she noted, "it would give us a head start in a big way."

He nodded quietly. "That's what I'm wondering about. The question is whether you will recognize anyone."

"Who knows?" She raised her hands, palms up. "However, I did see them, and I did talk to them, so there's a good chance the answer to that question is yes."

He stared at her for a long moment. "Fine, I'll arrange it with my boss." He looked down at his phone. "It is getting late. You were supposed to stay at home. Remember that part?"

"Yeah, remember that part about not being able to get ahold of you and knowing that Wendy was in trouble?" she asked. "So I came."

"Yep, you sure did." He sighed. "And then you got into an altercation with some guys looking for property potentially worth millions of dollars."

"Well, you know, if I'd seen the ring in person, I would have known because I certainly do know jewelry. But … I never saw the ring."

He looked at her keenly for a moment and nodded. "And you don't think she would have left it here?"

"I wouldn't think she'd let go of a multimillion-dollar ring. Except she has two goons after her. So not thinking she'd leave it here is a different story," she replied. "I had already wondered if the woman hid it here or hid it outside or tried to do something along that line. Maybe she darted in here to lose whoever was following her," she suggested quietly. "And maybe that didn't work out so well. The lady went out the back door, as Wendy said, and maybe lost it out there. Although I would more likely suspect she hid it out there instead, planning to come back and retrieve it."

"Hiding it out there in the alleyway would make more sense," Mack noted, "and we will check."

"Good luck with that," Doreen said. "I already have." At that, he spun and glared at her. She shrugged. "Before today, this case wasn't of any particular interest to you, so what was I supposed to do? Leave Wendy in the lurch?"

"Right." He smirked. "I mean, can't do that, or your next check might not come."

She frowned at him. "That's not fair. I don't have many friends in this town. I know a lot of people, but I am just on a cordial basis with them. So, for my friends, I would like to at least keep that much of a relationship going with them, like Wendy."

He nodded. "I didn't mean it that way. Well, I guess I did, but I didn't mean it. I was just teasing."

"Still, it's a valid point though," she agreed grudgingly. "I do have enough money to get through this month. I'm not sure about next month though."

He added, "Every month you've said that, and every month something has come up to help you, so keep holding the faith."

"Sure," she groaned. "Easy for you to say."

He smiled at her. "You're doing awesome. Don't give up now."

"No, not planning on giving up," she stated. "At least this way I don't think about my ex anymore." At that, he turned and looked at her, one eyebrow raised. She hurriedly explained, "Meaning, I don't worry about him coming to the door or trying to approach me," she stated for clarity's sake. "Obviously I'm not *thinking*-thinking about him."

He stared at her a little longer and then slowly nodded his head. "I would hope not."

She grinned at him. "Why? Are you worried?"

"Do I need to be?" he asked in that same low tone, studying her intently.

"No, not on my account," she replied. "I've already told you what kind of a loser he was. *Is.*"

"Maybe. But I also know that women have a tendency to change their minds and to do all kinds of crazy things that a lot of us men don't ever understand."

At that, she burst out laughing, making the others inside the store stop and turn and look at her. She immediately tried to calm her laughter. "Hey, right back atcha. We women don't understand you men either. But you already know that I'm fast becoming the local crazy lady."

There wasn't a whole lot he could say to that, and so he nodded. "Now would you please go home, take the animals, stay out of trouble, and I'll arrange for you to come take a look at some of the mug shots tomorrow morning."

"Sure." Doreen dragged Mugs away from Mack's ankles, where he had been sitting, waiting for attention like always, and then she called out to Goliath, who had taken up residence on a window seat. As she walked over to coax the big cat to come with her, she looked outside and murmured,

"You've got quite a crowd outside, Wendy."

"*Great*," she replied, "but the cop cars will scare away my business."

"Or it'll bring them in," she suggested. And, with the animals in tow, she opened the front door and walked outside.

Several people asked, "Hey, what's going on?"

She just called out to everyone, "Wendy's having a wonderful sale." And, with that, she made her escape.

She wasn't sure if it would help or hurt Wendy, but no way Doreen would tell the public anything of what was truly going on. Especially not if people knew that a reward may be offered for finding this diamond ring. That tidbit would get everybody and their dog out there looking for it. And that wasn't such a bad thing, but there was also a criminal element involved, and that would cause trouble too. She didn't want anybody getting hurt on her account.

With Mack's words ringing in her ear, she made her way home, where she once again locked herself into the house and planned to stay for the night.

Chapter 12

Thursday Morning

THE NEXT MORNING Doreen woke, bounced out of bed, checked on her time, and realized that she had two hours before she had to be at the station. Mack had texted her the previous night and had asked her to be there at 9:00 a.m. Since it was only 7:00 a.m., she had a long wait. And that would get frustrating too because she wanted to go now.

As soon as she finished feeding her animals and had her own breakfast—which she had to share with her furry and feathered crew as well—she settled down to go over her research notes, but there was very little to go on. Candy's engagement ring had never been seen again. And what were the chances that the ring Wendy saw was the same one? There were such things as fakes. Good ones. That looked very real. Besides, the yellow diamond from ten years ago showing up again after such a long absence just made no sense, especially the part Doreen kept coming back to, where there was absolutely no reason for anybody to go into Wendy's secondhand shop to sell that pricy ring.

Unless that woman had gone into the shop earlier and had placed it there herself. And the only reason to do that would be if she were being followed and needed to hide it there and then would retrieve later? Or ... the woman was in the process of hiding it at Wendy's shop?

At that, Doreen straightened. What were the chances that Wendy had approached this woman, maybe in the act of retrieving the ring or trying to hide it, and then the woman made up a crazy statement about trying to sell it as an excuse for being in Wendy's secondhand clothing shop with such an expensive piece of jewelry?

As Doreen sat here, pondering that latest hypothesis, her phone rang. She looked down to see it was Mack. "Hey."

"Any chance you can come in a little earlier?" he asked. "I've got a bunch of interviews later this morning. I'd like to get through these pictures first."

"Yep, no problem. I was just killing time until I could come down anyway."

He chuckled at that. "You do know that most people would hate to come. Yet, in your case, you're excited to do this."

"I am," Doreen agreed, "and I have a couple other questions I need to talk to Wendy about too."

"Why?" he asked, his tone sharp. "I need you to stay out of this investigation now."

She bristled. "You might *need* me to stay out of it, but I have a new line to tug. At least a new theory."

"Tell me when you get down here," he stated, "and we can talk about it then. But I do need you to stay out of it, as it's now an active investigation."

"What for?" she asked.

"They threatened her."

"Sure they did, but, other than that, I'm not sure you have anything else to work with."

"If you've got something to work with, then I have something to work with," he noted quietly. "And I'm serious. I need you to stay out of it."

She sighed. "You take away all my fun."

He burst out laughing. "You know that's not fair."

"I know a lot of things in life aren't fair," she muttered. "And sometimes you're one of them."

"I know you are just sulking and not actually thinking I'm unfair, so I'll ignore that comment. Now come on down," he repeated. "And let's get through these mug shots." And, with that, he rang off.

She sighed, got up, made her way to her keys, and told her animals, "I'm sorry, but you guys need to stay here." Then she reconsidered it and added, "You know something? No, that's not fair. You've been down to the station with us before. I'll bring you anyway. Mack can just deal with it."

With all the animals packed up and excited to be heading off on a field trip, she drove carefully down to the police station. Once there, she parked, unloaded all the animals, made sure Goliath was on a leash as well—even though he gave her one of those looks that clearly conveyed how much he didn't appreciate it. As she entered the front door, she looked over at the receptionist and asked, "Would you tell Mack that I'm here, please?"

The woman looked at her and all Doreen's animals and shook her head. "Oh, he'll be thrilled."

She shrugged. "Hey, they've been upset by all the goings-on lately. What was I supposed to do? Leave them behind?" The woman sniffed, and Doreen realized that she didn't have a fan in the front desk receptionist.

As she waited for Mack to come and get her, she wandered around, looking at the pictures on the walls. There was even a picture of Mack from a couple years ago. She smiled when she saw it.

Mack took one look at her and sighed. "Why'd you bring the animals?"

"Because they were upset at the thought of me leaving," she replied immediately. "Besides, it's a good idea for people here to have a better relationship with them."

His eyebrows shot up at that, and he just shook his head. "Come on. I've got a room for us."

She tapped the picture on the wall. "That's you, isn't it?"

He looked up and nodded. "Yeah, from a few years ago."

"You looked cute back then." At that, he stopped, turned, and frowned at her. She burst out laughing. "Sorry. I don't mean that you don't look cute now," she quickly backtracked, but the lady at the receptionist desk was already laughing. Doreen added, "Okay, so I mean you were cute then and now."

He just rolled his eyes. "Let's go."

Still trying to formulate a response that would make him not angry at her, she followed him quickly, the animals trying to get ahead of Mack. "Come on now," she told Mugs. "Behave yourself." He woofed at her and was quite excited to be led into another room. "He's always happy to see you," she replied. "I think he's a man's dog."

"And yet"—Mack turned to face her—"he's been yours all the time, hasn't he?"

"Yes," she agreed, "but the only other male he really knew was my husband as …"

Mack shook his head. "*Great.* Don't go comparing me to him."

"Nope, can't do that. But you know, from Mugs's perspective, that's the only example he had of a male. So it makes sense that he prefers you now because you're a new example of what a man should be."

He looked over at her and grinned. "Well, if you were trying to make up for your earlier comment, you just succeeded."

She looked at him, blinked several times, and then beamed. "I did, didn't I?" She nodded. "I get it right sometimes, not very often"—she sighed—"but I do get it right every once in a while."

He burst out laughing. "I'll be right back." And, with that, he disappeared.

She sat down at the table and wondered if there was any chance of getting a cup of coffee.

When he returned, he had coffee in his hands. He placed a cup down in front of her. "Now I'll go grab the books." When he appeared once more, he had the physical mug books.

"Why isn't it all digital?"

"It is digital, at least a lot of it's digital," he replied. "We'll start with these, and then we'll move to digital." And he began to flip the pages.

She took a look, shook her head, he flipped a page again. "This will be better if I do it." She took the book from his hands and turned it around so that it faced her. And she carefully checked each picture, turned the page; checked each picture, turned the page; checked each picture, turned the page, sipped some coffee, and repeated the process.

By the time she got to the end of the first book, she stated, "Nope, not there." And she kept on going through the other mug books. By the time she'd viewed all four books, she looked up at him and shook her head.

He nodded, got up, and left, returning with a laptop.

"Now take a look at these."

She went through a few more and shook her head, shook her head, shook her head. By the time she got done, she was quite depressed. "I guess it's a long shot anyway, isn't it?"

"We still have a couple hundred more faces," he stated.

She stared at him in astonishment.

He shrugged. "No, they're not all local criminals."

She snickered. "What'd you do? Raid the Vancouver database too?"

"Technically we have access to it all," he noted, "and, when you think about it, a heist like that would probably end up down on the coast anyway."

"Not to mention that's where Candy's from."

At that, he stopped, stared at her, and asked, "She is?"

Doreen nodded. "That's where her family is. I presume that's where she went to, after her engagement was called off."

"Maybe." Then he frowned. "Is that what you would do?"

"Depends how close I was with my family. If I couldn't stand them, then no," she replied. "But, when I ran into trouble, the only place I had to come to was my grandmother's. So that's why I'm here. I think women tend to be creatures of habit, and we go back to the source, when we're in trouble. It's kind of like when women have babies, and they tend to start healing their relationship with their parents, usually between the ages of twenty-five and thirty. Up until then, it's all hands off, and who knows where relationships end up. When they start having babies, they return to their own birth family again. And, no, I'm not making it up. That's a fact."

He raised both eyebrows. "You have the weirdest facts in

your head."

She grinned at him. "Sometimes, yep." She kept flicking the pages on the digital screen, using the mouse. By the time she'd gone through another thirty-odd pages or so, she stopped, focused on one photo, and frowned.

Mack got up, came around, and asked, "This guy?"

"I'm not sure," she stated quietly. "Something's very odd about him."

"Sure," he agreed, "but odd doesn't mean guilty."

She nodded slowly. "No, doesn't mean guilty but he does look very familiar." She tapped on his face a couple times, trying to picture him in real life. "I'm not sure that I saw him, but I feel like I saw him somewhere, somehow."

Mack sat down on the opposite side of the table and just looked at her.

"What?"

"You do realize what you just said, right?" After a pause, he added, "You want to clarify that statement?"

She frowned. "Okay, so I don't think he was one of the two guys with the van. Yet I feel like I saw him."

"Saw him where? Saw him when?"

She shook her head slowly. "I can't remember."

"The trouble is, we've also had a lot of cases that maybe this guy was involved in too." He pointed at the laptop. "You keep looking through the digital photos, and I will mark down that number, and we'll give you printouts to take home with you, in case it triggers some recollection later."

"Fine." She kept going for another twenty minutes or so, then she yawned and asked, "Any more coffee?"

"Maybe," he replied. "Are you getting anywhere?"

"I'm getting somewhere. I'm just not sure it's of any help." She went through a few more pages and stopped, clicked on one photo, and brought it up so it was larger. "*Him*," she said immediately. "He was the passenger in the van, not the driver. He didn't say much. Matter of fact, his threats seemed harsher than the guy in charge, the driver." She frowned, as she thought about it. "He was kind of like that silent heavyweight in the back."

"Got it." He read it his name. "Samuel Crispen."

"That's an interesting name too," she noted. "I can't imagine there being too many Crispens around."

"Not sure there's any," he replied. "It's not a name I know." He flipped the laptop around, wrote down the photo number, and then told her, "Okay, keep looking. You're still after the other guy."

She nodded, but, feeling better now, she kept clicking through these digital mug shots. Finally she came to the end. "I didn't see him."

He nodded. "That's fine. At least we've got one of them, so we might find the other one."

"And what are the chances that he could have come from, say, Alberta?"

"Definitely could have," he agreed cheerfully. "It is a challenge all the time with our investigations."

"Right." She nodded. "There really should be a global database."

"There are all kinds of databases," he explained, "but, if he isn't in one, it's quite possible he's not in any of them."

"Meaning, he may have so far not been caught."

"Possibly," Mark frowned. "And he could be somebody who has been on someone's radar but never been charged, as he's been working under the radar so far. Or maybe operates under one or many different names or ..." He shrugged. "Sometimes they can change their looks pretty dramatically."

Doreen perked up. "Now that's true. The van driver did wear a hat, and yet he wasn't too bothered about me seeing him, which I thought was kind of odd."

"That's just because you've had enough criminal elements in your world lately that you're looking for even more suspicious behavior from everybody."

"If he were a thief or some kind of conman, you'd think he'd want his face hidden."

"Unless he had nothing to hide maybe," he noted, looking at her sharply. "In which case maybe none of this having to do with Wendy is even criminal."

"Maybe not." Doreen tapped the table. "But what he said to me about Wendy was definitely a threat."

"And that is something we can go on, but we have to find him first."

"Right." She let out a heavy sigh. "That's a different story. These guys seem to always find a way to disappear and to stay hidden."

"Not always. Plus we got a hit, even with running just a partial capture on the van's plates," Mack shared. "It belongs to a Rodney."

"Okay, Rodney who?"

Mack quickly worked his way through something on the laptop. Finally he brought up the info. "Rodney Stanfield." And he flipped the computer around, and there was a driver's license with a picture.

She stared at it. "That's him," she said. "That's him."

He looked at her and asked, "Seriously?"

She nodded. "Yeah, that's him. That's the driver. Rodney Stanfield." And then she asked, "What was the other guy's name?"

"Samuel. Samuel Crispen. Now we have Rodney Stanfield."

"Got it." She nodded again. "I don't know either of them. Don't know that I've heard either of their names before now."

"No, I don't know much about them either, although Samuel has a record for breaking and entry, plus hot-wiring vehicles and stealing cars."

"Oh, Grand Theft Auto," she noted. "He was probably raised with that game."

He looked over at her and shook his head. "I don't think it's quite so cut-and-dried to make that direct link."

"Never is," she admitted. "I just read that the police had a lot of trouble with people when that game became very popular."

"That was a long time ago. You know that, right?" he asked, his lips twitching.

She shrugged. "I didn't say it was recent news," she muttered. "Anyway, can I go now?"

"You can," he replied. "This is a huge help."

She beamed. "See? Sometimes I am a help."

"Sometimes," he stated, glaring at her. "Just maybe try staying out of trouble today, huh?"

"Oh, just for you, I'll try. Today."

And, with that, he groaned. "That's not what I meant."

"Maybe not." She chuckled. "But it is something I can probably guarantee."

"Yeah, and, the minute you say that, it goes down the drain."

"Maybe," she agreed, still giggling. She got up and spoke to her animals—who were now more than bored and tired of staying in a cooped-up room. "We'll all head home. Maybe stop off at Nan's for some tea."

At those words, Mugs barked at her.

"Yeah, you want to go to Nan's?" she asked. Mugs danced around and barked once more. "Come on. Let's go."

"Thanks for coming in." Mack smiled, as he led her out to the entrance to the station.

Chapter 13

ONCE OUTSIDE, RATHER than alerting Nan, Doreen decided she would just drive by and see if it was convenient to visit Nan. If she was busy, they would go home again. As Doreen parked at the Rosemoor, she stepped out and looked at all the pristine green grass and, once again, thought about the gardener who had hated it when she walked on the grass. She deliberately walked yet again on the grass, knowing she was flaunting the rules. Somehow it just seemed like that kind of a day. She'd lived such a sheltered life when married, where she must do everything "right"— per her soon-to-be-ex-husband—that whenever she did something like this, it gave her a sense of power.

"Probably how people ended up on a criminal pathway," she muttered to herself.

And that was foolish because she was the furthest thing from being a criminal. Although she did, according to Mack, give legalities a wide margin when it came to solving her mysteries. And she guessed he was right about that. Not that she tried to go against the law, but, every once in a while, she found the rules to be more of a suggestion.

As she walked around to Nan's apartment, Doreen

didn't see her grandmother on the patio. So she stepped over the flower bed to the patio and pulled out her phone and called her nan. "Hey, where are you?" she asked Nan.

"I'm at Richie's. We're playing cards. Why? Did you want to come down and visit?"

"If you're not busy, the animals and I are already here."

"Oh my. I'll be right there." And, with that, she hung up.

Doreen didn't have long to wait before her grandmother bustled through to the patio. She gave Doreen a big hug. "Look at you. And it's so bright and early in the morning."

"Not that early." Doreen laughed. "Besides, I had to go down to the police station this morning, so I figured, if I was up and out already, I might as well stop by for a visit."

"Well, you're always welcome." Nan looked at her and asked, "I guess that means you didn't bring any jam, huh?"

Her eyes shot wide open. "Seriously? Are you out already?"

"No, not necessarily out," she replied, with a sniff. "I just want to make sure you're not going through it faster than I can get some refills for myself."

She stared wordlessly. "Pretty sure you got six jars."

"Yeah, pretty sure I did," she admitted, "but I am used to hoarding them, and, so far, I haven't told anybody I even have them. Otherwise I'll lose those jars I have."

"Then don't tell anybody now or later," Doreen stated immediately.

At that, Nan laughed. "I won't, don't you worry. I know exactly what these people are like around here. No way will I ever lose a jar of that jam."

"Can't believe you love it that much," she muttered.

Nan stopped, looked at her, and asked, "Didn't you have

some?"

"Sure I did, but it's … jam," she replied.

Nan gasped, almost like Doreen had sworn in front of her. "It's not *just* jam."

She held up a hand. "Sorry, sorry. Guess it's not just jam." Doreen couldn't stop her eye roll. "At least you enjoy it. That's what counts."

"It does, indeed. Now let me go put on the teakettle." Very quickly Nan came back outside with a pot of tea steeping and a couple plates.

Doreen noted the plates and asked, "What are those for?"

"Well, you were down at the police station this morning"—Nan beamed—"and you haven't told me why. So I figured that a treat might be in order."

"Do you have treats?" she asked her grandmother in surprise. "I didn't give you any warning."

"I don't need a warning." She gave an airy wave. "Richie had taken a few items this morning to have later in his apartment. So, when I heard you were already here," she explained, "I snagged a couple."

"I don't want to take any food from Richie," Doreen stated in horror.

"Oh, don't worry. He got enough for everybody in the blooming building this morning. I don't know what's going on with that man sometimes. He just doesn't want to eat in the main dining room with everybody, and so he takes a whole plateful back to his room."

"Well, maybe he just wanted some peace and quiet to himself," she suggested.

"Maybe." Nan shrugged and sighed. "I don't know. I think he's, you know, getting a little bit down that road."

Doreen wasn't sure what *down that road* meant, but, from the look on Nan's face, Doreen was supposed to understand it. "You mean, down the Alzheimer's road?" she asked.

"Well, one of those," Nan replied. "Love him dearly, but, every once in a while, he does things that make me worry about his mental state."

"You know what? I'm pretty sure Mack would say the same thing about me," Doreen quipped.

For whatever reason, that appealed to Nan terribly, and she laughed uproariously. "And with good reason," she added, still giggling. "I mean, after all the trouble you get into? *Tsk, tsk, tsk, tsk.*"

"Says you." Doreen grinned.

Mugs interrupted them, as he went up on his back legs and sniffed the table.

"Oh, yes, I didn't bring you a treat, did I? How forgetful of me," Nan murmured, then disappeared into the kitchen. When she returned, she had dog treats, cat treats, and a little bit of birdseed. And, with all the animals cheerfully accepting all treats, Nan asked, "Now do you want to pour the tea, dear? And I'll pull out these."

As Doreen watched, Nan opened up the first of two containers and pulled out several croissants. "Lovely," she noted, her tummy rumbling. "I can always have another meal right now."

"I figured so," Nan replied, "but you don't get any of my jam."

She stared at her grandmother in amusement. "You know what? That's totally okay. I can do without jam."

"Good, because I plan to eat it all myself. Plus you've got lots at home." And Nan proceeded to eat Esther's jam right in front of her granddaughter.

Doreen was more amused than horrified, but she wondered at Nan's manners even at that. By the time Nan had had a croissant with jam, Doreen had already gone through two croissants without any topping on them. They both sat back. Doreen rubbed her tummy. "Thank you. That was great."

"Good, now tell me why you were down at the police station."

Doreen shrugged and knew she would have to tell Nan something eventually. "I was looking at mug shots."

"Ooh," Nan replied in delight. "Tell me more."

So Doreen explained what had happened at Wendy's place, without getting into a whole lot of detail about why the threats were made or what the two guys were looking for.

At that, Nan stared at her. "You have the darndest knack for getting into trouble," she stated in amazement.

"Yeah, Mack seems to think the same thing."

"You should be doing an awful lot more to keep him close to you," Nan added, her tone serious. "The way you get into trouble, you need somebody to look after you."

Doreen knew Nan didn't mean that in an insulting way, and yet she was of a generation where it did take men to look after the little women. Doreen didn't ever really expect her carefree and independent grandmother to believe in that. "I'm doing just fine," she said gently, "especially with the help of the animals. They have saved me as much as anybody. Or, at least, they have delayed the bad guys long enough that Mack has time to arrive."

"Well, you are safe and unharmed, until you aren't." Then Nan frowned. "And I know I shouldn't be worried, but if anything were to happen to you …"

"I know," Doreen agreed. "It would be tough on you, as it would be terrible for me if anything happened to you too."

"Which is why you'll be very careful, won't you?" Nan asked pointedly.

"Absolutely," she murmured. "And I'm not sure that there's any danger at all."

At that, Nan stared at her. "You were threatened."

"Well, the threat was against Wendy."

"That would be terrible too," she noted, "because would you even get your next checks?"

Doreen stared at her grandmother and winced. "I will admit to being worried about that," she replied, "and that's terrible because that little bit of money that Wendy owes me is nothing compared to what I would feel if the poor woman lost her life. Everybody knows Wendy, and she has many friends in town. And I'm sure a lot of other customers would lose a lot more money than I would."

"Sure," Nan agreed, "but, at the same time, you also need it the most, in my opinion."

"Well, thanks to you, I'm not on the edge of destitution again."

At that, Nan laughed. "That couple hundred dollars won't help for very long," she stated, shaking her head. "It'll get you through a week or so, maybe, but only if you're very careful."

"Believe me. I'm careful," she replied immediately. "I can't afford not to be."

Nan nodded. "You need to get some of that auction money in soon."

"Oh, you and I both know that." She sighed. "Just seems to be all these barriers to getting it."

"And then, when you do get it," Nan added, "you'll have

so much that you won't know what to do with it."

Doreen frowned. "That's a good point too. I will proba-bly have to talk to somebody about that."

"And then you'll have to make sure that you talk to the right people," Nan suggested, "because, if you think about it, the wrong one is likely to cheat you out of your life savings."

"Well, I'm pretty sure that won't happen," she stated. "I'll find somebody I trust. And I would trust *very* few people around here with that kind of money."

"At least make sure it's safe, and you don't go into any crazy investments, where you'll lose it all."

"Hope not," she noted. "Besides, I don't even know how much money we're talking about, so it's a moot point at this juncture."

"Maybe … and maybe not. I just worry."

"And I love you for that too," she told her nan.

BY THE TIME Doreen and her animals made it home, she was tired. When she checked her watch, it was only noon. She unloaded the animals from her car, unlocked the house, stepped inside, and looked down at Mugs. "You know something, Mugs? I think we need a day to relax. Read a book, sit by the river, and just play." She picked him up, swung him around in her arms, gave him a big kiss, before setting him on the floor again. All excited now, he barked and jumped up around her.

She walked into the kitchen, put on the teakettle, and stated, "Now, the rest of the day to relax. That's perfect. Okay, so an afternoon at least. Maybe that'll be enough."

She made herself a big cup of tea, and, grabbing a

book—plus her laptop, her pad, and pen—she went to the back door, propped it open, and said, "Come on, guys. Let's go." And she led the way down to the river.

If nothing else, it was good for her soul to sit here and to relax and to just enjoy life for a little bit. She wasn't sure she could do anything on any Wendy avenue, not even Esther's trash-diggers complaint, at least not yet. She now had names to go with Wendy's goons though. At the thought of that, she wrote them down quickly and opened her laptop and figured, *What the heck? I might as well take advantage of this time. I can do some research, while we're all down here.*

And down on the creekside bench she sat, cross-legged with her laptop, and she quickly entered the names, trying to get some history on these two men. On the one guy, Rodney, she found next to nothing. He was out of Vancouver, which went along with what Mack had discovered. And of Samuel, she found almost nothing online for him either. When she researched just their last names, however, she found a different story. She had something on Samuel's family but nothing on Rodney's.

As she studied Samuel's relatives, she noted a connection to the girlfriend who had been engaged to Bernard. Candy was a cousin to Samuel. At that find, she quickly sent the information to Mack in an email. And then followed it up with a text, saying, **Connection between Candy and Samuel.** And then she returned to her research.

Now that she had discovered a connection here, this case was getting exciting. She wondered about contacting the family and seeing if anything was there to go on. But she didn't really have anything to ask yet. Doreen was interested in the history of Candy because it made more sense to think that Candy herself might have had the ring in her possession—if not since the failed engagement some ten years ago, then maybe recently.

If that were the case, where was Candy now? As Doreen searched the net, she couldn't find any mention of Candy. Frustrated, Doreen pulled out her phone and checked for phone book listings. And found what could be Candy's sister. In Vancouver.

Doreen frowned at that and quickly dialed her. When a woman answered the phone, Doreen explained who she was and stated, "I'm trying to get a hold of your sister Candy."

"You and the rest of the world," she replied bitterly. "She's AWOL for like ten years now."

"Oh my, you mean, like missing, as in police-case missing?"

"Nope, not at all. She told us that she was too devastated over the breakup of her engagement," Candy's sister explained. "And that was about a decade ago. She took off, and we haven't seen her since."

"Did she say she was leaving town and where she might be heading?"

"Yeah, that she would go away and think about what she wanted to do with her life now, and then we never heard anything more. So, if you find her or hear anything about her, could you please let us know?" She paused, then asked, "And, besides, why do you want to know?"

"Well, the diamond ring issue has come up yet again."

"Oh that," she groaned, with a note of disgust. "The worst thing anybody ever did was put a reward out on it. Everyone and their dog was looking for it."

"Well, I guess I have a couple more questions," Doreen stated. "Did you ever see the ring in person?"

"I did," she stated in a bored tone. "And, if that's what

your phone call is about, then I really don't have any time to talk to you."

"Maybe," Doreen admitted. "I just wondered if it was real or if maybe it was a really good imitation."

At that, the sister laughed. "If it were a really good imitation, I wouldn't know the difference," she declared. "You'd have to talk to Bernard about that. I mean, he's kind of cagey and more of a cheater than anything anyway."

"Do you think your sister really loved him?"

"No, she sure didn't. She was in love with the lifestyle, and I know that loss is what devastated her the most. And his accusations that she had stolen the ring and had sold it."

"Would she even know who to sell it to?" Doreen asked.

"No, I don't think so. My sister is a lot of things. Opportunistic, yes, is one of them, but she was also pretty naïve and innocent. If somebody told her it was worth ten thousand dollars, she'd have believed him."

"And would she have sold it for ten grand?"

"Nope, not at all because, with that ring on her finger and Bernard on her arm, she was worth a lot more than that."

"So she knew the value of having that man as her husband. And yet, through all this, the relationship didn't last."

"No, he broke it off because he was pretty sure that she'd stolen the ring."

"But that doesn't make any sense to me. Why would Candy steal it after their engagement? She already had possession of it. There was a notice in the local paper, with a picture of the two of them, and she wore the ring then."

"Well, that was part of the problem. And, knowing my gold-digging dingbat sister, I wouldn't be surprised to learn that she had lost the multimillion-dollar ring and just told

Bernard that it was stolen. Who knows? Candy could equally have hidden the ring, told her fiancé that it was stolen, just so he would buy her a second one."

The sister sighed loudly. "Of course I didn't say all that to her. If I had, I knew our own relationship would end. And look at that? Candy left regardless. However, I did tell her that I thought Bernard was just using the missing ring as an excuse to get rid of her, and she was pretty upset at the idea."

"But," Doreen interrupted, "that sounds like Bernard stole the engagement ring. Surely a man of wealth and experience, like Bernard, could break up with Candy, demand the ring back, and go on with his life."

"Oh, I didn't mean that I thought Bernard stole her ring back. In her own way, I think Candy cared for him. And she was pretty upset at the breakup. But, because she also really loved the lifestyle, it was hard to know whether she was upset about losing Bernard or upset at the thought of losing the lifestyle. The relationship and any communications back there did get a little murky—between Candy and Bernard obviously, but also between my sister and me. Once the innuendos and accusations started flying, it was pretty hard to sort out any truth or facts from lies and fiction."

"Right," Doreen agreed. "That gets ugly quickly, doesn't it?"

"It sure does," the other woman stated. "Anyway, if you hear anything about my sister, please let us know. We've been worried about her."

"So you haven't heard anything from Candy in the last ten years?"

"No, nothing," she confirmed. "Believe me. At the time, it also brought up some family accusations about maybe Candy did steal the ring and took off with it."

"And yet she would have gotten a lot more if she'd had married him."

"Exactly," the sister replied. "And that's why none of us really believed she stole it. She would get so much more if she had gone the distance."

"Well, I'm sorry for your sister if she's in trouble," Doreen added. "Hopefully she found something in life to make all this go away and to have a better future for herself."

"I hope so," the woman said sadly. "We have missed her. She was always a bright, bubbly, joyful woman, and I think that's why Bernard was really attracted to her. Just something about having her in your life made you feel good. But, once this all went down, I know she was pretty traumatized. And she did clearly say that she would disappear and that nobody should try to contact her and that, when she was good and ready, she'd contact us."

"Right, I'm sorry." And, not knowing what else to ask, Doreen added, "Thanks for talking to me."

"Wait, hang on a second," she said. "Are you the woman who does all that detecting in Kelowna?"

"Some of it, yes."

"Oh my," she replied. "So are you searching for my sister or the ring?"

"I'm trying to help somebody, who has been threatened over that ring," she explained quietly. "The ring doesn't interest me as far as a ring, except that it's a mystery that needs to be solved, and people are likely to get hurt over it."

"A lot of people were hurt in the beginning," the sister confirmed. "So I'd hate to see it come back up again and become yet another nightmare."

"I think it's too late for that," she murmured, "because, for some people, it already is too big a nightmare."

Chapter 14

DOREEN LOOKED AT the notes that she'd just written down, yet all of it added up to a whole lot of nothing. She went back to the beginning, rereading her research notes from the library, certain that something in there meant more than the others, if she could just find it. As she started to think about Candy and all the reasons why Candy might have taken the ring and run, a couple really good reasons were pretty obvious. As Doreen sat here, she had to wonder if this Candy person wasn't the same woman who had tried to sell the ring to Wendy. Doreen picked up the phone and called Wendy.

Distracted, Wendy asked, "Can I call you back?"

"Sure," she replied and hung up. At least Wendy didn't sound like she was under any pressure—like somebody was in the back, terrifying her. Doreen waited and waited and then waited some more for Wendy to return her call.

Finally Wendy called, and her voice was tired but excited, as she explained, "Sorry about the delay. And I may have to hang up again," she warned, "if it gets busy. Apparently all the publicity has been good for business."

"Well, there you go," Doreen said. "When you think

about it, any publicity is supposed to be good publicity."

"I don't know," Wendy argued. "In this day and age of the internet, somebody can kill your business pretty fast."

"Probably. I don't know a whole lot about that," Doreen admitted honestly.

"So why did you call?" Wendy asked. "And I'm not kidding. It's seriously crazy busy here."

"I was just wondering, thinking about all the things that have gone on at your place. And it occurred to me that maybe the woman who came to you trying to sell that diamond was Candy."

"Well, it's possible, I guess," Wendy suggested. "I certainly haven't met her before, and I highly doubt, given the clothing she wore that time, that I would have."

"Unless she tried to sell clothing to you," Doreen offered. "Once the engagement was over, she might have needed the money."

"Right, but that would have been a very long time ago, and I didn't have the store then," Wendy explained. "So, unless she's been hanging on to her clothing, kind of like you and Nan with Nan's clothes, that wouldn't have happened."

"That's a good point," Doreen admitted. "And you noted almost immediately that the woman was in a disguise?"

"Yes," she confirmed.

Doreen hesitated and then asked, "Is there any chance it was a male?"

At that, Wendy laughed, and then she stopped. "I ... I don't know. I would have said female, but I was going by all the usual trappings, so I don't know. I know that some trans people do a great job of looking female. So I'm ... I'm not sure. I guess it's possible. I didn't really get a good look at her. I was distracted by her disguise, then by her story, and finally by the ring itself."

"And do you think she'd ever been in the store before?"

"The police asked me that as well," she noted, confused. "I don't know what difference that would make. But I don't know. I do have a woman who helped out a couple days last week because I had a lot of issues with my parents, and I needed some help at the store. So she comes in every once in a while. I mean, it's possible that same woman came in one of those days. … I don't know." Wendy frowned, shaking her head. "I mean, if she did a different disguise each time she visited my store, maybe I wouldn't have known it was the same woman. I'm not exactly somebody who polices her customers."

"No, of course not," Doreen agreed. "It's just something that's playing around in the back of my mind. I mean, it wouldn't make any sense if it were Candy. That woman would have known the value of the ring."

"Right," Wendy stated quietly.

"Anyway, sorry to bother you. Go back to your clients." Doreen chuckled and quickly hung up the phone.

She sat here for a long moment. That hadn't helped at all, and yet, at the same time, maybe it had. Never occurred to Doreen that maybe Wendy's mystery visitor was a male, but it was certainly possible. Some guys were absolutely dynamite at makeup, so anything was possible, but was it likely? That's where it always came back to. What was this all about?

Doreen thought about Candy and what Candy's life must have been like. She was engaged. She's young. She's affectionate with this older man and knows that she's hit easy street. The ring goes missing—whether lost or stolen—and then her life falls apart. So what would Candy's motivation have been to steal the ring? It would have been better financially to save her engagement. However, if her engaged life was about to fall apart, then stealing the engagement ring made more sense.

Or did she take the engagement ring for herself, knowing that she could give it back, depending on who was at fault for the breakup? Doreen wasn't sure there was a protocol involved in something like breaking off an engagement, but, if he caught her doing something inappropriate or had a reason to break up with her, then he could easily have asked for the ring back. He could have just forcefully taken it back also.

And that was another aspect to this that Doreen wondered about. What were Candy's other relationships and friends like? Did she have a lover on the side, and then Bernard got wind of it and broke off the engagement, not wanting to be taken for a fool, even before he got married. It was certainly possible. Doreen frowned, wondering if it was likely though. She quickly phoned Candy's sister back.

When the sister realized who it was, she asked, "Oh God, will you be doing this all the time? Calling me multiple times during the day?"

"Sorry," Doreen apologized gently. "I'm trying to get an understanding of who Candy was."

"I don't know what difference it makes and don't use the past tense," she snapped.

"I'm using past tense deliberately, not because I think she's dead but because I ... I know that the person I was some ten years ago is very different from the person I am now."

The sister stopped for a moment and then grudgingly admitted, "Okay, that makes sense. ... Back then my sister had a lot of growing up to do. She was really excited about the rich life in front of her, but not everybody in her world was terribly happy."

"That, I guess, is one of the questions I have to ask. What are the chances that she had a boyfriend, lover, at the same time?"

"She'd have been a fool if she did," the sister replied. "No way that her future husband of hers would sit back and let that happen."

"That's why I'm wondering. Is there any way that she did have somebody in her life?"

"Well, she's had this friend that she's been close to for decades," her sister shared. "They were in school together. After high school graduation, they both went off on their own, but she never really walked away from him. We told her many times to ditch him. He was a loser. He had a prison record too, for lifting cars when he was a kid."

"You mean stealing?"

"Yes. He used to hot-wire them and take them and sell them to chop shops."

"Ouch."

"Exactly. Not the kind of people Candy should be hanging out with, particularly if she was jumping into a new life."

"No, Bernard wouldn't have taken very kindly to that.'

"Supposedly she had broken it off with him. And wouldn't see him anymore."

"And did you believe her?" Doreen asked Candy's sister.

"No, not at all," she admitted freely. "I warned her that she would mess up her life completely if she didn't get rid of him, but I know that he had—they had—a very strange relationship, and, when he called, she came running."

"Right. Is there any way that she would have come running if he had called her at the end of that messy, broken engagement?"

"If he had called her at the end, after everything was stolen and she'd been broken up with, absolutely she would have gone to him," she stated, with complete confidence. "But she wouldn't have done it before. And I think that long-time boyfriend was totally happy to have her with that old guy, thinking either that she'd kill him through their sex life or that he'd just die of old age and then this old friend could step in and scoop up the benefits."

"Nice guy," Doreen noted.

"Yeah, in a way, there was always just the two of them, even when he was off doing his thing. When he was in jail, she would just shrug and say, *He'll be out soon*, and Candy would carry on meanwhile. He'd be out, and then she'd be all over him again."

"And you think the other guy was totally okay with Candy marrying Bernard?"

"I don't know about *totally okay*," she replied carefully. "But Candy and I did have an argument or two about him still being in her life, while she was engaged. At one point Candy did break it off with this boyfriend, and I was really happy to hear that. However, at the same time, I wasn't sure that he would be gone for good. Up until now, he hadn't been gone for good at any point in time."

"Interesting that some people have relationships like that. They know they're bad for them, but they just can't stay away."

"That was them, although I'm not sure that I would agree that she knew he was bad for her. She was just someone who couldn't say no to him. The two of them had been so close for so long that, in a way, they should have just stuck with each other."

"Do you remember his name?"

The other woman laughed. "Good God, how could I ever forget. Joel. Joel Timber. The guy's a jerk. He's a chauvinistic conman. And he had my sister always wrapped up."

"And have you heard from him? Did he contact about your sister? Anything like that?"

She hesitated for a moment. "Not in the last few years, no."

"And what about early on, when she said that she needed to disappear for a while?"

"No, I didn't hear from him then. It didn't occur to me that she had gone with him at the time. She would have. Yet I still think she would have told me, if that's what she had done," she replied quietly.

"Depends on where this guy was at during that time, right? Was he in jail? Was he free? Was he with somebody else?"

"I don't know," she stated. "I hated the man."

"And did Candy know that?"

"Oh, she knew that. No way she couldn't have."

"So maybe she wouldn't have told you then because maybe she knew you wouldn't approve."

At that, the sister fell silent. "I hope you do find out what happened. Now you're making me feel guilty that I didn't do more."

"Not at all," Doreen rushed to say. "But I do want to find her or at least find out what happened to her. If she chooses not to come back or if she can't come back because she's no longer with us, that's a different story. Hopefully, at least, if we have the truth, everybody can move on."

"And what's in this for you?"

The other woman's suspicion was well-founded. "A friend of mine has been threatened by a group of men over the engagement ring," she explained quietly. "So I'm just trying to help my friend."

"Right, you mentioned something about that before."

"Exactly. And, as often happens in these cases," she noted, "it's important to go back to the beginning."

"Well, in that case, I sure hope you've talked to Bernard because, if there was ever a beginning, he's it."

"In what way?"

"He found Candy when she was at work at a grocery store, swept her off her feet, and didn't give her a chance to even think about saying no. Before Candy understood what was going on, she was flying with the higher echelon of society, dressed in diamonds and jewels, and treated like a princess. It was complete nectar to a girl like Candy, who was starving for bigger and better things in life. She was positive that she would get all that gold and glitter. And I'm pretty sure that Bernard just helped fuel that sense."

"Maybe," Doreen noted, "and it's not all that unusual a story. An older man sweeps up a younger girl, plies her with all those lovely gifts to make her realize just how her life would be like when married to him, and, before you know it, they are married. But it's not always that way. It often happens in reverse."

"That could be," the sister said, "but I don't think so in this case. My sister always wanted bigger and better things, and dear Joel," she explained, with a note of sarcasm, "always promised her bigger and better things but always failed to produce. However, when it came to Bernard, I'm pretty sure Bernard fulfilled all his promises to her and just kept pushing more on her."

One thing Doreen had learned from that second phone call was quite correct—she needed to connect with this Bernard person. Unfortunately she didn't know who he was, and, chances were, if he was as wealthy as everybody said he was, he was probably well-guarded. She knew what that meant. Her ex-husband had always had this whole army between her and the public. He talked to who he wanted, when he wanted, and nobody else got even within hearing distance if he didn't say so. And that was likely to be the problem with this Bernard guy.

She frowned as she considered that.

Then, realizing she was getting a headache, she told the animals, "Mugs, you want to go for a walk?"

He jumped up and started barking, running around and chasing his tail. She wrote down the address that she had, but it was only the subdivision name, no street name and number, just a general description, and it wasn't likely to be enough for her to pinpoint Bernard's house. But, if she could get close enough, she might work her way into talking to him. It wouldn't be all that easy.

Yet she had a lot of experience dealing with guys like her husband, so maybe. Of course, hopefully this guy was a whole lot different than her husband. Somebody needed to be; the whole world couldn't be that bad. Still, even to attract his attention, given what she'd read about him, she would need a little bit more ammunition.

And, with that, apologizing to Mugs, saying, "Just give me a minute to get changed," she headed upstairs.

Chapter 15

WITH MUGS ON a leash, Goliath running along beside her, and Thaddeus curled up on her shoulder, complaining the whole time, she headed down the river to all the properties along the lake. It was just one of those things generally thought of the high and mighty as living on waterfront properties. Yet some megamillion-dollar properties were up in the hills behind as well. She couldn't be sure, but there was some mention about Lakeshore.

Now Lakeshore was down and around the corner, but she'd gone along the river and across an access path. There were cut-offs over to Lakeshore Road and definitely some spaces where she could get to the beach, but walking along the beach—although it was supposed to be available to the public—wasn't always that easy to walk along without encountering barriers.

A lot of people had put up docks to try and discourage the public from walking on their beachfronts. She was pretty sure they weren't allowed to do that, but, hey, it was kind of standard for places like this.

As she headed along the lake, she cut back along Bluebird and continued to walk. Lakeshore could go two directions, and this was one of them, and it went all the way down to where it split—half heading down along the lake again and the other half of the traffic going up the hill to Upper Mission. An awful lot of traffic headed in that direction. She knew it was popular because the views were absolutely to die for.

In her case, however, she was looking for some of those very large properties a little farther down the road. As it was a gorgeous day, and she thoroughly enjoyed the walk, she quickly realized that she had gone a bit farther than she'd intended to.

Frowning, she stopped at the entrance to a street called Hobson and waited for it to click in her brain as being one of the richer well-to-do areas. With a nod, she headed down there. As she walked, she passed several other people. One lady was walking a dog in a carriage. Doreen stopped to admire the dog.

"He's old," the woman shared, with a gentle smile, "but I just can't put him down yet."

"As long as he's not suffering, why would you?" she asked, with a bright smile. "He looks totally happy."

"He is, indeed."

The older lady seemed grateful maybe for the conversation but definitely was not up for somebody judging her. "Matter of fact, is he friendly?" Doreen asked. "I'd love to pet him."

"He's quite friendly," she replied.

At that Doreen squatted in front of the carriage and talked to the dog. His tail wagged multiple times. Mugs, not to be outdone, jumped up beside her and stuffed his nose over the top of the carriage to sniff the dog. "No, you're not getting a buggy like that at all," Doreen told him firmly.

The other lady laughed. "This is your dog?"

"It is." She smiled up at her. "We've been together all of his life too. It'll break my heart when it's time for him to go."

"I think it breaks all our hearts, unless we're old and ready to go." She shook her head. "It seems like such a waste to lose anybody young. And, of course, if we are blessed to have our pets until they are a ripe old age, it just is sad because it's not the same ripe old age that we want them to be, like ours."

"Now isn't that the truth," she agreed. She slowly got up and stared down at the dog, a gentle smile on her face. "I only have my grandmother now, and I know that'll be a hard time when it's her time to go."

"If she's had a good life …"

At that, Doreen smiled and nodded. "She is having a great life. Anyway, I have to keep walking."

"Are you going somewhere specific?" the other lady asked her inquisitively.

"I was looking for Bernard Pertel's place."

"Oh my, that's just down a couple more houses. So you're almost there."

"How would I recognize it when I get there?" she asked curiously.

She gave Doreen a broad smile. "Everybody's got gates, but he's got … *gates*."

At that, she laughed. "Right. Of course." She gave an automatic eye roll. "Thanks."

And she turned and kept on walking. She turned around once to check on the older lady's progress, but she was still working her way down the street. Doreen headed down Hobson, not surprised that he would live here. Not surprised in any way, as she walked past the houses. They were stunning. She'd lived in similar houses with her husband, but those days were long gone.

And, even now, she wasn't sure that she would want to leave Nan's place. It was special in ways that she couldn't really explain. It was a sanctuary for her. And something that Nan had offered her without any conditions to help her get back on her feet. And, for that, Doreen would always be grateful, and the house would hold a special place in her heart. She couldn't even imagine renting it to somebody because what if they damaged it? If they didn't treat it with respect, she'd feel terrible.

Nan, of course, would probably tell her to stop being foolish and to sell the old thing; it was worth money. But Nan knew how to make a quick buck off of anything, apparently. She did better even while she was in the old folks' home than Doreen was doing out in the real world. And how did that figure? But then her grandmother was involved in some things that were a little questionable. Not that she minded, as her grandmother was full of heart, and, if anybody needed money, she was there to help them out. And you had to love that.

Doreen kept on walking, passing what appeared to be more beautiful, more beautiful, and even more beautiful houses. It's almost like they had a competition going around here to see who could build bigger, better, faster, higher. She almost laughed, but she passed one property that looked like it must have belonged to a geologist or something because massive rocks were out front.

Then she approached another place and stopped. Yeah, okay. So everybody had gates along here, but, wow, this guy had *gates*. Stone gates with almost a medieval thing going up and down each side. The place was stunning from the outside, but it must be even more stunning, she imagined, on the inside. No way she would get in there to talk to him either. She frowned, as she stood here.

The gate suddenly opened in front of her, and a Jaguar pulled out. One of the latest sporty things. Wow, it was nice. She stepped out of the way, smiled, waved a hand, and kept on walking. She added a little bounce to her step as she walked. She wasn't sure just how available this guy was and just how desperate he might have been. She almost chuckled at that.

But when a man called out, "Hey," she turned and looked in his direction.

There was an older gentleman, standing outside his car, walking around it now, with white hair and a huge girth.

She walked back over to him. "Hey, sorry, did you say something?"

"Were you looking for something?" he asked. "It looked like you were looking at my gate."

She smiled. "Well, that depends." She laughed. "I'm investigating the disappearance of that lovely diamond ring."

He rolled his eyes and went back to his car. Just then Mugs started to bark. Bernard looked down at the basset hound. "Hey, do I know you?"

"I don't think so," Doreen replied, walking forward a couple steps. "I haven't been in Kelowna all that long."

He thought about it several times. "No." He shook his head. "Weren't you involved in finding a bunch of jewels in town here?"

"Yep, sure was. That was a cold case and a half."

He laughed at that. "A friend of mine was telling me about the jewels you recovered."

She nodded. "Yes, and I'm grateful that we managed to find some closure for that couple as well."

"No kidding." He looked at her with a newfound respect. "Now you're looking into ... my diamond ring, huh?"

She nodded. "I was hoping to, but trying to get answers from people? That's not ... always easy."

"Nobody wants to talk about it," he replied. "Particularly me."

And she smiled at the grumpy tone to his voice. "That's because your heart got broken at the same time."

He sighed. "My heart always gets broken. I fall in love very quickly, and I don't always make the best choices as to women."

"I think that's part of falling in love, isn't it?" she asked him gently. "I mean, when you fall in love, it's the fall that's the most fun."

He looked at her, and then he started to laugh. "Oh my, you are a pistol."

She raised her eyebrows at that. It's a phrase her grandmother would have used, but not one that Doreen was totally thinking as appropriate for her generation. Yet, as she looked at him, she realized that he was probably closer to Nan's age than hers. She smiled. "If you've got a few minutes, it would help a lot to get a few more details."

He sighed. "Well, you'd better get in then. I'm heading up the road. I have a business deal I must talk to somebody about. If you've got time to come with me, I'll answer your questions on the way."

"Sure." Then she looked down at her animals. "As long as you're okay with the animals getting in your car."

He smiled at Mugs. "I'm totally a dog lover. Now I'm not sure about the cat."

"And how about the bird?" she asked, flipping back her hair.

His eyes widened as he saw Thaddeus. "Now I know it's you. You always have the animals with you, don't you? And they help you solve the crimes." He started to rub his hands together in joy.

She wasn't sure if it was because he was thinking of his diamond ring or because he had just confirmed who Doreen was or if something else was going on. She nodded. "Yes, that's me."

"Get in. Get in," he said. "I haven't had anybody interesting to talk to in at least a week."

At that, she burst out laughing, and he grinned at her.

"I mean it," he stated. "Everybody here's *boooring*."

Chapter 16

AND AGAIN DOREEN laughed. "As long as you're okay with the animals." At his nod, he opened up the passenger door, and she saw a blanket on the back seat. Mugs immediately hopped up there, and Goliath even joined him. The two of them just sat up and looked at her expectantly. "Good enough," she told them. "Now stay on the blanket." And then she took the front passenger seat.

Bernard looked at her in surprise. "Are they that well behaved?"

"No," she replied bluntly. "Just when you think they're that well behaved, they go off and do something that lets you know they are in no way behaved at all."

He nodded and smiled. "In that case, good. You know you always have to be suspicious of people who think that their animals are perfect."

"Oh, mine are not perfect," she confirmed, "but they are mine."

At that, he smiled, shut her door, and got back into the driver's side, and turned on the engine.

She was well accustomed to expensive cars, as it had been one of her husband's pastimes. But she could appreciate the quality and the luxury of this model.

As she settled back in her seat, he asked, "Comfy?"

"Oh, absolutely," she said, with an airy wave of her hand. "This is a nice model. The last one I was in was I think maybe the model before this one." He raised his eyebrows. She shrugged. "My ex."

"Ah, exes are good for that, aren't they?"

"Not a whole lot else either," she noted in a caustic tone.

Again he burst out laughing. "Oh, I do like you."

And that was the first glimpse she had that she might be in trouble. She stayed quiet as he drove.

Finally he looked at her and asked, "Now what were all those questions?"

She nodded. "Did you have a relationship issue with Candy before the diamond went missing?"

"Yes," he stated bluntly. "Found out she was still seeing that no-good friend of hers."

"Right. Joel by any chance?"

He frowned and then nodded. "You have done your homework."

"I'm trying. It's really the only way to get to the bottom of these issues."

"And yet the police didn't," he muttered.

"They probably did, but they don't have enough man-hours to do all the investigations needed. And I do find that, after a few years, the passage of time tends to loosen people's tongues. Whereas back when the incident happened, they're afraid of getting in trouble, and they stay mum."

"Well, I was certainly loquacious about what happened," he stated, "so I don't know that I had anything to stay mum about. But, when I said I fell in love, I wooed her like I've never wooed anybody else. She was the sweetest thing."

"Was?"

"Was." He gave a dipped nod. "No, I don't know what happened to her, don't know anything about her, haven't had anything to do with her since," he replied. "But, when you fall out of love like that, you fall out hard."

"Right. Nothing like a dead love."

"Oh, yes," he stated. "I agree with that wholeheartedly. And that just makes me very sad. I love the process of falling in love. I love being in love, but the aftermath, the reality afterward, is just awful."

"Maybe you shouldn't fall in love quite so easily," she suggested, with a raised eyebrow.

"No, you're quite right. I should have done more due diligence. I should have taken it slower. I should have done all kinds of things that I didn't do. But what can I say?" And he flashed her a beautiful smile. "I love women."

She burst out laughing. "Okay, I'm forewarned."

He nodded. "So you should be. You're single. You're beautiful. You're smart, and I like that."

"And yet Candy appears to have been not that smart."

He chuckled. "You see? Candy had something that you don't have."

"And what's that?" she asked curiously.

"She was innocent. Innocent, innocent, innocent. She didn't understand how the world worked. She didn't understand very much about real life at all. At the beginning that was sweet, unique, and I felt very almost paternal toward her—of course paternal with, you know, a difference."

"Of course. Nothing like a nice young *thang*," she replied, with a twang, "to bring up the old hormones to stand up and scream hallelujah."

He chuckled again. "Nope, and nothing is wrong with

my hormones. And back then she just hit the spot. *Um, um, um.*"

She smiled at that. "And then what happened?"

"You know that it takes a while to really understand who's who in a relationship, and I got her locked into an engagement while we found it out because I didn't want her going off with somebody else. That's when I realized that some of the people in her past weren't exactly as clean as I had hoped."

"And that maybe she wasn't quite so innocent as you thought?"

He winced at that. "I was really hoping that you wouldn't have picked up on that, but I will admit that I was a fool, and, according to my friends, I was an *old* fool," he admitted sadly.

"Back to that whole concept of, when you love, you love deep, and you love long, and you love hard, and then you are outta love."

"Exactly. I jumped in. It was a great time for everyone— and then it's not."

"Sorry," she said gently.

He looked over at Doreen and grinned. "Hey, I'm just glad that I can talk about it now without getting angry."

"Did you get really angry at the time?"

"I sure did," he shared. "At the time, I'd been completely snookered. That ring had been incredibly expensive. But I was okay with it because, well, she was the one."

And there was his self-mockery in that tone, enough that she turned and looked at him. "And when it disappeared?"

"She tried to tell me that it was stolen, but I was pretty sure that she'd taken it."

"But that logically didn't make any sense."

"No, it sure didn't."

"Because it might have been worth a lot, but surely being your wife would have been worth a lot more over a longer time."

"Exactly. I was always very generous. None of the women in my previous relationships ever would have said anything other than the fact that I was generous. It's just being generous wasn't always good for me."

"Of course not," Doreen agreed. "And then, when you get angry, what are you like?"

He shook his head. "I can get very angry," he admitted quietly. "But I'd never hurt anybody. I do have a roar," he confirmed, shamefaced. "And I deal with businessmen all the time, so you must have an edge in business. You should be fair, but you also need an edge. If you don't, the world will walk all over you."

She'd seen it herself and knew what he meant. "I get it, but was there any reason for her to be afraid of you?"

"Nope, not at all," he stated. "Have you talked to her?"

"Looking for her right now. Even her family hasn't heard from her since right after the breakup."

He frowned at that. "I mean, I wasn't very nice at the time because honestly, I was sure that she had stolen the ring, yet she was telling me it was missing."

"Now tell me something," Doreen said. "Were you the one breaking up? I understand there's a certain etiquette in who keeps the engagement ring when breaking up. That she gets to keep it if you're the one breaking up with her, but, if she's breaking up with you, I think she's supposed to give it back."

"Wouldn't have mattered either way because I was breaking up with her because of her own bad behavior—

having an affair with a previous boyfriend of hers—and I definitely would have gotten the ring back," he murmured. "It was worth millions."

"And was it insured?"

He paused and then nodded. "Yes, it was. Not a lot of people asked me about that."

"My ex had a lot of expensive items, and everything was insured."

"And so then what's the next question?" he asked, a smile playing around the corners of his mouth.

"Whether you had an imitation made?" she asked quietly.

He looked at her, smiled, and replied, "I certainly did."

"Of course you did," she stated. "Good, I'm glad that you were smart enough to do that. So how did the real one go missing?"

"That's the problem. Our fight was rather public—in my home, during our engagement party—and she made a rather dramatic gesture of throwing the ring away. And then she took off. As in, disappeared from sight. Of course I figured she'd taken the ring and run as far and as fast as she could, and honestly, she did a good job of hiding the ring and herself from me."

Just enough disgruntlement was in his voice that kept her from smiling at someone besting him. Like Doreen's ex, men like Bernard didn't think much of losing.

"But the imitation could have been on her finger, and she threw that one away, having the original stashed elsewhere?"

"Oh, I thought about it," he noted. "Believe me. I thought about it." He looked like he wanted to say something but held back.

"And did she know it was fake?"

He nodded. "She did. I told her that."

"But she might have thought that you just said that in order to upset her."

He shook his head. "I'm pretty sure she knew she wore the fake that night. She threw it at me during this public fight of ours, and I lost my temper because lots of people were there. And when she chucked the ring, anyone could have picked it up—keeping in mind that not everyone knew this was a fake. But we did a full search of the premises and the guests. The only one I didn't get to search was Candy, as she took off right away."

"Right," she murmured. "So losing the counterfeit ring itself wasn't necessarily the problem."

He nodded. "Kind of changes things, doesn't it?"

"Maybe." Doreen frowned. "Did Candy have access to the safe?"

"No," Bernard replied. "Not at all."

"You didn't trust her?"

"It wasn't about that, not at that time, but we weren't living together yet," he explained. "That was due to come, and, of course, the blinders came off very quickly."

"Right." Doreen considered all that. "And what about security?"

"Of course I have high security, both physical guards and digital technology," he confirmed. "Anybody in my position does."

She nodded because she'd seen that firsthand too. "So really, it was an inside job."

"That was my take on it," he noted. "And I know exactly who was the inside person."

"And you think she gave Joel access?"

"I do." Bernard looked at her in surprise. "You're good at this."

"Well, I'm narrowing it down to potentials," she stated. "And I do have a tendency to see that, when all else doesn't make any sense, what's left is something you have to seriously consider."

He pondered that statement of hers for a moment. "You know what? I would have possibly been okay with her trying to steal the real diamond if she had just told me the truth, but, because she kept denying it, and it ended up in a big mess—breaking and entering, lying and theft, and all that affair stuff—it became quite an issue. And I have to admit. She broke my heart."

"And have you been engaged since?"

He shook his head at that. "No, she was the one who stopped me from falling in love anymore."

Doreen shook her head at that news. "Sorry to hear that. Sounds like maybe it is time."

"Maybe." He nodded. "Doesn't mean I liked avoiding falling in love. As I said earlier, there's something very joyous about being in love."

"Well, there is about the journey," she clarified, "but remember the other part, that awakening part on the other side?"

"No, you're right. That's not so joyous," he agreed. He made several corners up ahead and then pointed. "I have to pull into here. I won't be long."

He pulled up, parked the vehicle, took the keys with him, making her smile because, of course, that was another trust that he probably no longer had the same level for anymore, and he hopped out.

Doreen turned to Goliath and Mugs, lying quietly on

the blanket on the back seat. "You've been so nice during this trip. I'm sure Bernard thinks so too. When we get home, I'll give you all something S-P-E-C-I-A-L." She chuckled, as she couldn't say "treats," or her animals would demand those now.

Thaddeus perked up, shook out his wings, and said, "S-P-E-C-I-A-L. S-P-E-C-I-A-L."

"Wow, Thaddeus. I've never heard you spell a word." She pet her beautiful African Grey parrot. "But are you just repeating what I said, not really understanding what I meant, right?"

Thaddeus rubbed his beak along her cheek. "Thaddeus loves Doreen. Thaddeus loves Doreen."

"And Doreen loves Thaddeus and Goliath and Mugs." She chuckled and gave a quick thanks for her many blessings. "I'm sorry I don't have W-A-T-E-R to give you guys. We'll do that when we get home."

Thaddeus fluffed his wings and added, "W-A-T-E-R. W-A-T-E-R. At home. At home."

"Yes, at home. Wow."

She sat here quietly, as she thought about what Bernard had told her. Joel was obviously the first person anybody would blame, particularly if Candy continued to have a relationship with him, even while engaged to Bernard. Obviously she was betrothed in word only. But it didn't make any sense that she would steal the real diamond engagement ring—an overt act, surely to be noticed by Bernard, as versus the supposedly covert act of having an affair with Joel. Why would she steal either version of her engagement ring, unless she was planning on taking off immediately thereafter? And the only person who could tell Doreen more about that would be Candy herself.

But then why come to the secondhand store? *Ever.* Yet, even more curious, why come ten years later? Why try to fob off the diamond ring there? Even if it were the fake version, it would have been a very good imitation, and even selling it for $10,000 would have been still cheap. And then Doreen had to wonder, maybe it wasn't about the real diamond? Maybe it was about the imitation diamond ring? But why? She considered this conundrum for another twenty minutes, not getting any answers, or at least not any logical ones.

Bernard came back, half running. As he got in, he said, "Sorry about that. I didn't expect the meeting to be quite so long."

"That's fine." Doreen waved her hand. "I have just been thinking about all the information you shared."

"And did you come up with any answers?"

"Some. How much was the imitation ring worth?"

"Oh God," he replied, "that was expensive too. Maybe ten thousand plus?"

She smiled and nodded. "Bingo," she stated under her breath.

He gave her a sharp look. "Why?"

"Because that confirmed one part of the story," she noted. "And one part that I might solve. Now the fate of the real engagement ring, however, that's a different story." She looked at him and frowned. "Are you still in the same house, the same safe, the same everything?"

He nodded. "Yeah, why?" he asked. "Believe me. I've turned the house upside down and backward. The real engagement ring is not there."

She nodded. "Maybe not. And did you ever have any break-ins afterward?"

"A couple." He nodded. "They were all chased away.

Why? Are you thinking it's still in my house?" he asked, with a note of outrage.

"I'm not sure yet," she admitted. "I'll have to think on this a bit more."

He stared at her. "You know something? You're kind of scary."

"Yeah, I am," she agreed. As they drove along the road, she added, "And don't you ever forget it."

He looked at her in surprise, and then a beatific smile crossed his face. "I like you."

"*Uh-uh-uh*," she replied. "You might like me, but I'm not available."

Immediately his face fell. "What does that mean?" he cried out, as if brokenhearted.

"I have somebody special in my life, and I'm still trying to get rid of a husband, from a legal standpoint," she explained. "So, no, that's not happening."

He stared at her for a long moment. "Are you sure?"

"Absolutely, positively," she stated. "I get the whole attraction and that whole love thing, but I'm pretty sure a lot of other women out there are missing a beautiful opportunity because you've taken yourself off the market," she noted. "You might just want to put yourself back on."

He smiled at that. "Maybe." He shrugged. "But you know what? Trying to find that person, the one who makes you feel that way, that's a different story." And again he turned and looked at her.

She shook her head. "Nope, nope, nope, nope." She laughed. "Don't look at me like that."

"Well, I'll keep it in mind," he teased. "Besides, I won't let you get too far away. You're too smart, and you obviously have a line on what's going on here. So this is something where I'll keep close to you regardless. Now," he said, "do you want me to take you back where you were walking? Or will you come and have a drink with me?"

"You can drop me off at my place," she stated, knowing he would have no problem finding out where she lived regardless.

"Perfect," he replied. "Will you invite me in?"

"No." She laughed again. "But, if you give me your phone number, I'll stay in touch over this case."

"Oh, absolutely," he agreed.

When they finally pulled up in front of Nan's house, he looked at it and asked, "This backs onto the river, doesn't it?"

She nodded. "It sure does. I absolutely love it."

He nodded. "Whoever bought this made a very wise financial decision back then. This was a good investment." He pulled out a business card and handed it to her. "I appreciate what you are doing regarding this matter surrounding my broken engagement. Even if you don't find the ring and only find Candy, even if you don't go out with me"—at that, he laughed—"please keep me in the loop."

"I can't guarantee that I will solve any of this," she clarified. "However, I will definitely have more questions, and I might need access to your house."

He studied her and realized she was serious, and his humor fell away. "Anytime. I would really like to have answers to this, once and for all. I do feel like it's held me back."

"It absolutely has," she agreed gently. "Don't worry. I'll do my best."

After exchanging phone numbers, she got out, moved all the animals out with her, and walked up to her house. As she turned around, she heard the lovely purr of that Jag headed down the cul-de-sac. He honked twice and then disappeared around the corner. When she turned back, she found her neighbor Richard, standing on his front step, glaring at her.

"What's this?" he asked in a suspicious voice. "Is that ex of yours back?"

She shook her head. "No, absolutely not, that was Bernard Pertel."

His eyebrows shot up. "The developer? What on earth are you doing with him?"

And such surprise filled his voice that she had to admit to bristling slightly. "What's wrong with me?" she asked. "It's not like I'm chopped liver."

He looked at her blankly for a minute, as if not understanding the *chopped liver* reference. And then he snickered. "No, but you're not exactly cream pie either."

And, with that, he went inside and slammed shut his front door.

Chapter 17

Friday Morning

T HE NEXT DAY Doreen was still fuming about Richard's cream pie comment. She'd poured some coffee down her throat before going outside to get some mental therapy by beating up on the dirt. She took her temper out on the weeds in the backyard garden. She finally came back inside at 9:00 a.m., hungry, as she hadn't even eaten yet.

Of course she had fed her brood hours ago. No getting around that. Otherwise Mugs would bark and prance incessantly back and forth between her and the pet food cabinet. Even worse would be Goliath, weaving between her legs, preventing her from even getting to the cabinet—which just proved a cat's contrarian attitude. The last thing she needed was to break a leg or whatever by tripping over her huge Maine coon cat, possibly hurting him too. With a shake of her head, she was thankful that Thaddeus was the most patient of her pets, yet he could be the most vocal.

As she stepped back into the kitchen and washed her hands and face, she put on a second pot of coffee and sat down on the deck, tired now but a little bit calmer.

When her phone rang, she looked down to see it was

Mack. "Hey. What's up?"

"I'm five minutes away. Any chance of a coffee?"

"I just put a pot on," she noted.

"Oh, good." Doreen noted the fatigue in his voice. "Normally by this time you've already drunk a pot."

"I have," she admitted. "I'll see you in a few minutes."

He drove up, while she stood at the front door. She let him in, noting how physically tired he looked. But he still sat down on the living room floor and cuddled Mugs, who was ecstatic to see him. And even her standoffish Goliath threw himself down on Mack's lap. When Mack stood up, Thaddeus hopped up his leg. After Mack put his arm down, Thaddeus continued up to his shoulder.

"This is what I needed," Mack admitted. "A welcome like this should always be in everybody's day."

"Well, it certainly is on my list," she shared, "but I don't get treated like that. I mean, I wake up, and they're usually in my face, squawking at me because they want food or out or something," she said, with a laugh. She led the way to the kitchen and poured two cups of coffee. "So how come you haven't had coffee yet?"

"How come you're just having coffee yourself?" he asked in response.

"I had coffee earlier, but I woke up in a temper. So I went outside and decided to take it out on something that couldn't talk back."

He raised his eyebrows, as he accepted the cup. "And what was it that couldn't talk back?"

"The garden," she stated succinctly. Then she gave him a bright smile and led him outside.

"So what got you in a temper this morning?"

She shrugged. "This case."

"What about the case?" he asked curiously.

"Well, tell me why you're here first," she replied.

He shrugged. "Not sure there's a *first* in this," he noted. "Just, you know, all kinds of crap going on in this city that I have to deal with."

"Right." She nodded, remembering that she wasn't privy to a lot of the stuff that did happen here. "I'm just working on the missing diamond case," she said, smiling up at him.

"Any progress?"

"Yeah, in a way, and, in a way, not." She recounted what happened the day before with Bernard.

His eyebrows shot up. "You got into the car? With a stranger?" he asked, his tone turning ominous.

She immediately glared at him. "Don't you start with me." She plunked down on the deck. "Sometimes you have to trust a little." Silence came from beside her, and she looked over to see Mack's face working. She shook her head. "I am not in the mood."

Finally he let out a slow releasing breath.

"Good," she noted. "Nice working on the control."

"Yeah, well, I wouldn't have to work on my control," he muttered, "if you would listen."

"Listening's one thing. Obeying? Well, that's a whole different story."

At that, he burst out laughing and looked at her affectionately. "I can't imagine you being married to your ex and obeying."

"Yeah, but that's because I'm not afraid of you," she replied immediately. "You won't hurt me."

His smile fell away. He reached across, wrapped an arm around her shoulders, pulled her into a hug, and whispered, "I'm glad you've finally come that far."

She sighed and cuddled in. "It's just a confusing case," she muttered. "Well, not all that confusing. I pretty well have it all figured out, just have a couple things left to sort."

At that, he pushed her away so he could turn her around, and then stared at her. "You what?"

She looked at him, raised an eyebrow, and said, "You heard me."

"I want to hear more about this."

"I won't tell you, not now," she said, shrugging. "I don't have enough information yet. Once I lock it all down, I'll tell you." He frowned at her, and she frowned right back. "You tell me about your case."

"I can't," he declared, glaring at her.

She smiled. "No, I get it. That's okay."

"No, it's not okay," he argued, "because you'll beat me to death over my silence."

She chuckled. "I would never hurt you. You know that, right?"

He sighed. "You are a challenge."

"Good," she noted. "Nothing good should ever be easy."

"Maybe," he admitted, "but it would be nice if *some* things were easy."

"No, that's true," she agreed. Then she groaned. "Nan gave me a couple hundred dollars, so I need to get some groceries."

"Good idea," he replied. "Why don't you pick up something that you want to cook, and I'll teach you. Maybe tonight? If I can get loose from work. I'll let you know."

"That would work," she agreed. "I'm not sure what to cook though. I hadn't realized just what a chore it was making a decision every night about what to eat." His lips twitched. She glared at him. "Don't you even say it. I know that I lived the entitled life before. However, that's not the point here."

"Nope, it certainly isn't," he noted. "And *entitled* doesn't mean *free*. You were definitely not free."

"Nope, I wasn't," she confirmed. "And I haven't heard from him recently, and I haven't heard from your brother again either."

"That's a good thing. Let them duke it out."

"Will there really be *duking* though?" she asked fretfully. "You know my ex doesn't play fair, right?"

"We know that, both Nick and I," he stated. "And, yes, I know that your ex's dangerous, which is also why I'm trying to get you to stay safe."

"I'll stay safe," she replied, yawning. "Besides, I mean, after being told I *wasn't cream pie either*, that's an insult that I'm still trying to get over."

He chuckled. "Honestly? Sounds like it's not a bad thing."

"Says you," she argued. "I don't know what, but something's going on with Richard."

"For you, something always going on with everybody."

"Yeah, but he's … different."

At that, Mack just nodded. "He's definitely unique, but that doesn't matter."

"Maybe not," she stated. "At the same time, he is a conundrum."

"*Uh-oh*, that just means you'll try and figure him out."

"If he hasn't done anything, I can't really figure anything out, can I?" she asked, raising both hands in frustration.

"It sounds like you're waiting for him to do something, so you can get into his life and tear it apart."

"No, I don't want to do that," she stated. "Something's

sad about him. I don't really want more sadness in my life."

"Is this case getting you down again, like the others?" he asked, frowning at her. "Remember? You have to take this work in small doses."

She smiled. "Yeah, how about we try paddleboarding or something fun again coming up? To take my mind off all this stuff."

"Perfect," he said. "Dinner tonight, and then we can go out paddling tomorrow, no better make it the day after."

"And we make a day of it," she offered. "We can go out paddling on Sunday and have dinner Sunday night."

"And that works too," he agreed. "Considering the work I've got, maybe that's better," he admitted. "It may end up being Monday even."

"Good," she replied. "I need to spend some time with Nan too."

"I'll let you know." He looked around. "Hate to ask, but you got anything to eat?"

She laughed. "I've got toast. And jelly."

He looked at her in surprise. "I haven't had jelly in a very long time," he shared in delight.

She rolled her eyes. "And I didn't even know it was a thing until a couple days ago."

"It's not only a thing," he explained, "it's a heritage thing, especially when talking about Esther's jam. But quince was never very profitable commercially, so it wasn't something that anybody ever turned into something you'd find in the supermarket," he noted, "but that doesn't mean that it's any less viable."

"Well, if you say so." She got up off the deck, walked back into the house, and then returned. "I do have bread and jam, and I even have peanut butter."

"I'll take it," he said, standing up to join her in the kitchen.

She watched as he put four slices of bread in the toaster. "Wow, you are hungry."

He nodded. "I am. I'll buy you another loaf of bread later."

"No, you won't. You've fed me more than enough times."

As soon as the toast was done, he buttered all four and put peanut butter on half, and then she handed him the jelly jar. He looked at it, and his eyes lit up when he saw it. "Is this *it*?" he asked almost reverently.

She watched in astonishment, as he took the knife, dipped it into the jam, and then tasted it. He closed his eyes and almost swooned. "Good Lord," she stated. "Now I know why they say the way to a man's heart is through his stomach."

"Absolutely. But you can get to my heart anytime," he joked. And then he winked at her.

She flushed. "Now you're just joking," she replied, laughing.

"Oh no, I'm not."

"You have to be," she murmured. "You know what my cooking's like."

At that, he burst out laughing. "Good point." He slathered jam all over his toast without peanut butter and took a bite. He sat down right in place. "Wow," he muttered. "This has got to be Esther's quince jelly."

She stood here with her hands on her hips. "So not only can you tell that it's quince, you know who made it?"

"Only Esther made jam like this," he declared. "I used to go with my mom to the Kelowna market and get it from her."

"Wow. Well, it is Esther's," she confirmed. "She gave me several jars." He looked up at her hopefully. She sighed. "Apparently I didn't get enough jars from her though."

"No, there is no such thing as enough when it comes to this," he stated reverently. And he sat here in peace and just finished his first slice, then the second with peanut butter, and then again had buttered toast with jam.

She smiled at him. "I'm glad that you really enjoyed that." Seeing the look of joy on his face, she was happy that she could at least give him that much. She got up, walked over to the pantry cupboard, where she had put the jelly, and pulled out one jar, and handed it to him. "There. Now you can't say I didn't share."

He looked at the jam hopefully. "Is this another one?"

She nodded. "It is. And it's for you." He beamed like a little boy. She shook her head. "And you promise to enjoy it all?"

"Not only do I promise to enjoy it all," he said, chuckling, "I promise to not share."

She rolled her eyes at that. "You better not. I do not have enough to give everybody in town a jar," she exclaimed.

"Who else have you given them to?"

"Nan, and, boy, she had a similar reaction to you."

"We were all heartbroken when Esther stopped making it. I mean, we understood, but, at the same time, you know, she had a heck of a market built up."

"Sounds like she had a good thing going. She doesn't look like she's terribly flush with money, so I'm surprised she's not still doing it."

"I think it's hard work, especially for just Esther to handle alone," he noted. "And maybe she just doesn't care to do that anymore."

"Maybe. I know she told me that she had put away enough food for years and then amended that to say that, now that she'd reassessed her age and how much she had stored up, she'd put away enough for decades."

He frowned. "If you ever have an opportunity to get more, get *lots* more," he suggested, looking at her hopefully.

She shrugged. "She gave me enough that it would be suspicious if she were to give me more because I suddenly ran out," she noted. "I'm hardly drinking this stuff."

He looked at it and shrugged. "You know what? It'd be worth it. Can you imagine this with ice and some gin?"

"Nope, I sure can't." Doreen frowned and shook her head.

He grinned at her. "Well, you have definitely given me a trip down memory lane, and I will take the jar with joy," he declared. And he snagged it up.

"Now sit there and finish your toast," she said, as she walked over, grabbed the coffeepot, and topped up their cups. "And after you're gone, I might have a lie-down and just let some of this stuff run through my brain."

"At least you're not getting into trouble."

"Nope, I'm not," she agreed, "at least not at the moment." At that qualifier, he glared at her. She shrugged. "Hey, it's early yet today. Who knows? Maybe all kinds of things can still happen."

"But you said that you had a few more things to sort out."

"I do," she muttered. "Those will be a little harder. I need to find some people who are a little hard to track down."

He stared at her. "Are you thinking about Candy?"

"That would be lovely, if I could," she noted. "I'd even be happy to talk to the Samuel guy. Did you track him down yet?"

"No, we suspect he's gone back to the Lower Mainland."

"Yeah, that would make sense, but then they're probably doing regular runs up here. They must be, if they have hit Wendy's place already a couple times this week and last."

"Maybe." Mack sighed. "Anyway, I need to get back to work." He ate the last of his toast, looked at the coffee, and shook his head. "I might not have time to finish this."

"Then leave it, and I'll drink it," she suggested. "You might feel that way about the jelly, but I feel that way about my coffee."

He smiled. "Good point." He sat here a little bit longer, drank half the cup, and then groaned. "Damn, I have to go." He checked his watch. "Otherwise I will be very late." And, with that, he got up and headed to the front door, with Mugs trailing sadly behind him. Mack bent down, said goodbye to Mugs, and, still holding his jam jar, he headed out the front door.

She followed Mack outside and waved him off. Of course it looked suspicious to anybody outside to see Mack leaving her place midmorning, but like she cared. Besides, just enough people were watching her place that she felt inclined to give them a show every once in a while, just to keep them gossiping. At that, she turned and looked at Richard's place, and she noted a window curtain closing immediately, as if caught spying.

She laughed. "I might not be cream pie to you," she yelled, "but I'm sure not crab apples either."

And, with that, she marched back inside. She almost thought she heard Richard chuckling, and it put a smile on her face to be honest. She didn't think she was all that bad-looking, and she might not be a catch by the way of catches; but, hey, she'd done just fine. As soon as she had that thought, her phone rang. She picked up her cell, didn't recognize the number, frowned, but answered it. "Yes?"

"I don't want to give you that much money," her husband growled. "How dare you even think you deserve that much."

She smiled and immediately clicked the button to hang up on him. She didn't have to talk to him. But she sent her lawyer a quick message, saying Mathew had tried again.

At that, Nick called her back. "That's good. It means he's coming around to our way of thinking."

"But he said he doesn't want to give me that kind of money," she repeated. "How do you think that's coming around to our way of thinking?"

"It means he's ready to break. Do the same thing, if he calls you again. Just hang up on him and let me know each time he calls," Nick told her. "Believe me. This is progress." And, with that, he hung up.

Chapter 18

ALMOST AS SOON as she hung up from Nick, her phone rang again. She looked down, not recognizing the number, and when she answered it cautiously, she heard Bernard's voice.

"It's coffee time," he stated. "Come out and have coffee with me." His voice boomed through the phone.

She chuckled. "I'm having coffee now."

"Hah. Okay then, it's teatime. Come have tea with me."

"What's this for?" she asked. "I haven't got any further answers for you yet."

"Oh, but I like that," he noted. "You're not there *yet*, and that? That's good. I really do want to hear the end of all this."

"And what will that bring you?" she asked curiously.

He hesitated and then replied, "I haven't really found anybody since Candy," he admitted. "There's always been that sense of distrust."

"Of course, and, in your mind, she also took the ring."

"Yep," he agreed in disgust. "And once that trust is broken …"

"No, I get it," she murmured. "I really do. I just wonder,

if I don't find any answers for you, how will that impact your life?"

"I'll keep doing what I'm doing," he stated in a slightly bristlier tone. "I'm not a child."

"Of course you're not," she replied gently. "But you're right. I think it's holding you back."

"So then, find some answers for me," he stated brightly, "and then I'll move on with my life."

"I'm working on it," she noted.

"Well, if you don't want to go for tea and if you don't want to go for coffee, how about you come and see the house?" he offered. "That'll give you an idea of the lay of the land. Besides, you wanted to see something about it anyway."

"No, you're right, I do," she agreed. "Particularly where the safe is."

"The safe's in the bedroom," he noted, and then his voice dropped into a teasing tone. "I'd be happy to show you that."

She sighed. "Only if you keep your hands to yourself while we're there."

"You're no fun," he complained loudly.

But she heard the laughter in his voice. "Yeah, I've been told that a time or two," she muttered to herself. "Fine, I'll come down with the animals."

"You could leave the animals behind."

"Nope, not going to." She shook her head. "I come with the animals or not at all."

"In that case," he replied, "feel free. I'll expect you in what? An hour? And you can stay for lunch."

She laughed. "Man, give you an inch, and you'll take a mile."

"Give me a mile, and I'll take the whole damn town," he declared, and, with that, he hung up.

She smiled and then realized that she probably shouldn't be smiling. In her defense, she was still nursing the hurt from Richard's snide remark. And a harmless compliment can be accepted, without it going any further, right? With a sigh, she turned and looked at her animals. "Well, it is all in the name of our investigation," she muttered. Even Mugs looked at her with a raised eyebrow. "Okay, stop," she replied grumpily. "It's not what I would choose today either. But we have a chance to go look at Bernard's house, so we need to go take a look and see just what could have happened."

And, with that, she headed to her car, with her animals in tow, and this time Goliath wasn't terribly happy to be along for the ride. She pondered that, as she got out at Bernard's gates. Just as she went to hit the intercom, the gates opened right in front of her. She got back into her car and slowly drove forward. Somebody was at a security booth even farther down. She looked at him and smiled. "I'm sorry you have to sit here the whole time."

He laughed. "Not the whole time, but it's business," he noted. "For my workday, it's part of what I need to do."

She nodded. "Yeah, I do understand working." Yet she knew that they wouldn't see her "work" experience as anything compared to theirs. She'd been in that gilded cage, whereas everybody else was just working for the gilded cage.

As she drove up to the house, she parked off to the side, and, by the time she had the animals unloaded, she found Bernard standing there, a big smile on his face.

"You see? Even just seeing you," he said, "puts a big smile on my face."

"That just means that you're really suffering and need to

get out more," she noted drily.

He grinned. "People don't usually talk to me like that," he replied. "I always get that certain amount of deference here."

"Yep, understood," she agreed. "And maybe that's why I don't talk to you that way. It's kind of hard to have that kind of respect, when I've been here before."

He nodded. "Sounds like your marriage wasn't all that happy."

"No, sure wasn't. That's the whole reason for the divorce," she shared, with a smile.

"And you obviously didn't do very well out of it, if you're living in that small house."

She shrugged. "Even if I had millions, I probably wouldn't move out of it right away."

He looked at her and nodded. "Ah, you're sentimental."

"I absolutely am, and it keeps me nice and close to my grandmother. If and when it's time, her time to … to leave, I will make a decision at that point."

He nodded. "Is she in a home?"

"She's in Rosemoor."

"Ah, quite the characters are down there, I've heard."

"Yeah, and the ones who you've heard about are probably Nan," she admitted, with a laugh. "That woman can't stay out of trouble, no how."

"Sounds like her granddaughter came by it naturally then."

She laughed "You know what? You're quite right. And I wouldn't have it any other way."

He nodded. "Nothing wrong with having spirit." He shrugged. "I mean, I'm not as close to an old folks' home as some people might think. And it'll be a hard thing for me to head to."

"Yet you have money, so that maybe you would prefer to have a private nursing staff instead," she suggested. "You have options because of the money. But my grandmother is there because she likes people, because she likes having company. And I think, honestly, the last few years were tough on her, and this has put a whole new lease of life on her."

"I wouldn't be surprised, but I'm still a long way away from thinking about that."

She nodded. "Everybody wants to think they were miles away from assisted home living. But somehow those years just seem to pass so fast that you didn't really have a chance to adjust, and, next thing you know, you're in the same position Nan was in."

But Nan had been fully cognizant and willing to go to Rosemoor, when she'd made the decision to move in there, and that made a big difference. It was a choice for Nan. And a choice that Doreen well knew that Nan did not regret.

Mugs walked over with a certain amount of dignity to Bernard, who bent down and said, "He's a nice dog. I'm not so sure about the cat, but, hey, the dog's nice."

"Well, the cat's nice too," she stated in Goliath's defense, happy to see him cooperating with his leash today. "Neither of them are very nice if somebody sets out to do me wrong."

He nodded. "I have heard some tales about them," he admitted. "After meeting you yesterday, I had my assistant bring up some information."

She nodded. "Ditto." Immediately he straightened and looked at her in surprise. She shrugged. "And why wouldn't I?" she asked. "You're heavily connected to this case."

He winced at that. "As much as I don't want to be,

you're right, and I don't really have any choice in the matter."

"I don't know about that either," she clarified. "But it seems like you're definitely involved. The question now is, to what extent?"

"Well, I certainly didn't steal the ring myself," he muttered. "And, yes, I did get the insurance payout, but I'm not worried about money. In my position, I never have to worry about money again."

She nodded once more. "And you seemed to be pretty adamant about getting this situation solved now."

"Of course," he stated. "I wasn't kidding about it holding me back."

She studied him for a long moment. "No, I agree."

He looked at her with relief. "Hey, you're one tough cookie."

She laughed. "No, I don't think so, but I'm getting to be a decent read of humanity. And that's not always easy."

Immediately the smile fell from his face, and he shook his head. "That's the problem with doing business all the time. We live in a business world, and it's not necessarily a nice one."

"It doesn't have to be an ugly one though," she argued. "I don't understand why business has to be done in such a cutthroat way."

"It would be nice if we at least could go back to the handshake deals," he shared, "where you could trust somebody and what they said."

"True," she agreed. "And I've known quite a few people I would have liked to trust, but it just didn't work out that way."

"Ditto," he said and smiled. "Come on in." He looked at

the bird on her shoulder and shook his head. "I don't think I've ever seen a bird like that."

Thaddeus poked his head out from under her hair, stood up tall, and squawked, "Thaddeus is here. Thaddeus is here."

Bernard looked at her, back at the bird, and then laughed. "Good Lord, no wonder you're such fun to be around."

She shook her head. "I don't know about that. Just when you think you understand these guys, they do something that completely throws it all off."

"I imagine so. They must walk to different drummers."

"So do I," she noted. "It has certainly become something I've had to accept, as I don't really fit the norm for anybody."

He nodded. "You know something? Nothing's wrong with that. Sometimes the norm isn't what any of us want or need."

"Maybe," she replied, "but sometimes it's hard to understand just what we do need."

At that, he opened the front door and let her and her animals inside. She stepped into an absolutely gorgeous mansion of a house. She smiled, as she looked around. "This is lovely," she noted warmly.

He studied her intently. "Do you like it?"

She nodded. "What's not to like?" She threw her arms out. "If nothing else, just the wide open space is beautiful."

"That's what I thought," he replied. "I wasn't really planning on doing any kind of renos to it."

"Nope, I wouldn't either," she stated. "At least not until you're ready to."

"I don't know that I'll ever be ready to," he stated. "Seems foolish now to even think about it."

She looked at him in surprise. "Were you thinking about it?"

He shrugged. "Somewhat, yeah," he added sheepishly.

"Ah, a lady friend again."

He glared at her. "You make it sound like I don't make my own decisions."

She just gave him a raised eyebrow and asked, "Do you?"

He winced. "And again, I guess I kind of deserve that. I can't say that I was thinking that I was being manipulated or easily persuaded to do something, but maybe I have been."

"This house is very important to you," she noted. "I would only change what you need to change for your own comfort," she stated. "I hate to say it, but—you know, as evidenced in your life—partners come and go, yet the house remains here loyally ever after."

He stared at her and then slowly nodded. "I hadn't considered that, but you're right. The house has always been here for me. The people? Well, not always."

"Exactly," she agreed. "That's how I feel about my house. It's been some stability which I badly needed in my life."

"You were really hurt from the divorce, weren't you?"

"No, not so much," she explained. "The divorce was a good thing. The hurt was before that."

He winced. "I suppose he was one of those guys who had affairs."

"I don't know, don't care. He was one of those guys who had a heavy hand."

At that revelation, Bernard looked at her in horror, and she nodded. "Believe me. I was well-trained. I didn't get that hand very often. And this is a very private conversation," she declared, annoyed at herself for even bringing it up. "So I have to trust that you won't spread it around."

"Never," he agreed. "But, like you, I'm also very easy to talk to."

"Too easy," she muttered.

He chuckled. "Come on. Let me show you around."

And, with that, he led her through several rooms that were all incredibly beautifully decorated, and the ten-foot-tall ceilings were just something else to stop and stare at.

But when they got to the living room, and she noted the twenty-foot-tall ceiling, she blurted out, "Wow, hanging Christmas lights will take a really tall ladder."

He looked at her and laughed. "You do know that I don't hang them myself, right?"

"Right." She nodded, thinking back to the days when she hadn't had to either. "It's been a while," she admitted. "I had forgotten how much help it is to have money."

"Something I presume you don't have now."

"Not now," she agreed, "but I'll take what I've got now over what I had then."

"And what's that?" he asked curiously.

"Freedom."

After that, he just nodded. "Very wise, indeed." And he led her on a tour of the entire place.

When they got to the master bedroom, he said, "This is the master bedroom, and, yes, this is where the safe is. I actually have two safes."

"One in the office?" she asked. "Presumably the other one is there."

He nodded. "And it just makes sense, doesn't it?"

"It does, but then I also think that it makes sense then to a thief too."

He nodded. "I hadn't considered that, but, if you

guessed it, then I guess that makes sense, doesn't it?"

"It makes sense," she agreed, "but I'm not sure that it makes enough sense to go change it."

He pondered that a minute. "If I were to rebuild, I might change it, but, given the circumstances, I don't think I'll be rebuilding anytime soon."

"You never know," she noted. "A lot of life is left out there for you."

"Maybe. Building a house is a stress that I'm not sure I want."

"You've already built multiples of them," she replied, "so I'm surprised you would hesitate over building another one."

"Maybe. Maybe. I don't know. It's definitely not today's problem." And he smiled at her.

"So this is where the safe is. This was where the real diamond ring was, and the only other person who was regularly in the home at this time was Candy."

"Right."

"And did she know ... have access to the safe?"

He shook his head. "I might be a fool, but I'm not stupid."

It was her turn to laugh. "Right. What about your security guys?"

"Nope, nobody has access but me."

"So then I have to ask, where do you keep your logins and all that kind of information?"

"You're thinking that somebody got them off me?"

"No, but I'm saying that somebody got in here, and there had to be a way in."

"Sure," he muttered, as he thought about it. "I keep all that stuff in the office."

And she asked, "Have you opened it much, the safe?"

"Nope, I sure haven't, and it kind of makes me angry every time I see it."

"Might be another reason to build another house," she suggested. "When you think about it, that's a lot of anger to have to deal with too."

He shrugged. "Maybe, but it's also an awful lot of expense to have to deal with if I do build."

"Nope, got it. Anyway, where's the office? We must have passed it earlier."

He nodded and pointed. "It's on the main floor. Right underneath us."

She pondered that and walked back out to the hallway and looked down. "So somebody could have come up here, and, if they knew that another safe was down here, they could have hacked into both."

"Maybe, but nothing was missing, other than the ring. And a safe cracker is not exactly somebody you can just pick up off the street."

"No, I'm sure it isn't," she admitted. "They have to be very skilled, don't they?"

"Sure, and this is a pretty expensive safe."

"Meaning that you thought it was secure."

"Meaning, it *is* secure."

At that, she stopped, looked at him and asked, "Okay, so if it is secure, how did the ring get stolen?"

He flushed. "Okay, so maybe not that secure."

She hesitated. "I know this is tough. I get that. But, if we want to get to the bottom of it all, we need to have clarity here. Is there anybody else who would have had access?"

He immediately shook his head. "No. Honestly, I don't tell anybody this kind of stuff, particularly since then."

"But …" Again she hesitated and then pressed forward.

"You know that pillow talk's a great time for letting out secrets."

He nodded. "And I'm not an idiot. Remember that part?"

"Sure," she agreed. "Remember Candy?"

He flushed, and his glare turned slightly dangerous. Then he nodded. "You don't hold back on your punches, do you?"

"It's a little hard to do when we're looking for a ten-million-dollar diamond," she explained. "I mean, there is that saying about fools and their money are quickly parted. And, in this case, you have a safe in the bedroom, and you know that the real diamond ring was in there, so somebody had access. If it wasn't you and if it wasn't Candy, who could it have been?"

"My vote is for Joel," Bernard admitted, "but apparently, at the time, he was in Vancouver, just released from jail like the day before, which seems like a bad thing to do and so soon after getting set free."

She stared at him. "Now that is a piece of information I didn't know," she shared.

"I had a private detective on him," he replied silently, "who got Joel's phone number and traced its location. So it was unlikely to have been him—directly at least."

"Or he could have left his phone at home, while breaking into your safe."

"Or that, yes." Bernard frowned.

"You want to share that private detective's report with me then?" she asked. "It would help me to put the final pieces on this."

He turned to face her. "Final pieces?"

She nodded. "Yeah, final pieces."

"You mean, you've solved this?"

"Nope, not yet," she noted, "but I'm not that far off." He stared at her, dumbfounded. She shrugged. "I get it. I do. Not everybody sees things my way, but generally I can get to where I need to be fairly quickly."

He shook his head. "I would be absolutely shocked to find out that you had already solved this."

"It's not a case of already having solved this. More often than not, it's a case of people not wanting to tell the truth at the time of something happening because they're afraid of the repercussions. But, like I said before, over time, some of that fear diminishes, and you can get answers that you wouldn't have had previously."

"I'd really like to think that," he told her, "but it's a little hard for me to see how you could have gotten here so fast."

"Oh, I'm not there yet, but I am close."

He nodded slowly and stared at her. "In that case, I will absolutely send you a copy of what my private detective sent me, but I can tell you it doesn't say much. Joel went to prison, and Candy disappeared off the face of the earth. However, … hopefully it will help you put on the *finishing touches*, as you say."

She smiled at him. "Thank you."

Chapter 19

Saturday Morning

WHEN SHE WOKE up the next morning, she rolled over to an insistent phone ring. "Hello, Nan," she groaned into the phone.

"Oh," her grandmother replied. "Did I wake you?"

"Yes, you woke me," she said. "Did you have a reason for calling me?" she asked, yawning, turning over on the bed, so that she was propped up on the pillows. "What time is it?"

"It's nine a.m.," her grandmother shared in astonishment. "You never sleep late."

"No, I didn't get much sleep last night," she admitted.

"And does that have anything to do with your afternoon with the richest man in town?"

At that, Doreen's eyes popped open. "Oh, good Lord, I see the rumor mill is running overtime."

"It certainly is," her grandmother noted with satisfaction. "And you had the animals with you."

"Of course I did. I always have the animals with me." She yawned again and said, "Oh, man, do I need coffee."

"Of course you need coffee, but you should come down here and visit with me instead," Nan declared. "You can have tea here. I'll expect you in five, … in ten minutes." And, with that, her grandmother hung up.

It was hardly a request; it was more of a summons, and yet what did Doreen expect? Once the rumor mill got onto that latest tidbit, Doreen should have expected her grandmother to be calling. And hardly the richest man in town. But then she pondered that. Or was he? It wasn't an issue as far as she was concerned; she'd seen big money. She'd seen megamoney at her dining room table, and it still didn't impress her. People were people, and Doreen would just as soon not have much to do with any of them who are impressed simply by money, if she had an option. Not sure that Nan did, but, hey, that was just the way life went sometimes.

As Doreen pondered her next step, she got up and managed to get dressed and headed out, walking with her animals, feeding them treats along the way to Nan's. By the time she got there, she felt better, more alert, and was not yawning. The animals were more than frisky and delighted to be playing at her side. When Mugs saw Nan, he raced ahead, almost knocking Doreen over. "Hey," she called out to him. "Remember your manners." But he completely ignored her.

Nan looked at her and smirked. "Obviously you were a little late getting out of bed this morning," she noted, her eyebrows going up. "Is that what happens when you don't sleep alone?"

"Good Lord," she said, "of course I slept alone."

Nan's face fell. "But he's the richest man in town," she cried out.

"Like I care," she scoffed.

At that, Nan smiled. "I do love that about you. You're so

very honest."

"Maybe," she agreed. "But I don't know why all of you are fussing about who it was I saw yesterday afternoon. It really doesn't matter to anybody but me."

At that, her grandmother laughed. "And, if you believe that, you aren't using your brain."

"Meaning?"

"Meaning, everybody's interested in everything you do. You've become a celebrity in town, child."

"*Great*. You know I don't want that, right?"

"Well, you keep solving all these mysteries, and people keep coming to you for help, so, when they see you going into somebody's place like that, of course it'll raise some eyebrows."

"Yes, but it's connected to a case," she replied grumpily, as she sat down at her grandmother's table.

At that, Nan immediately perked up. "Oh my. Really?"

Doreen nodded. "Yes, really." And she yawned again.

"You really are tired, aren't you?"

"Well, I didn't sleep well. I had a night where everything just seemed to go around and around in circles," she muttered. "Nothing makes any sense. I know I'm really close to solving this, but, so far, it's just not there in my brain."

"Well, that has become a rather magnificent brain of yours," Nan pointed out, as she poured two cups of tea. "You should be treating it nicely."

She stopped and looked at Nan. "You mean that I haven't been treating it nice?"

Nan frowned. "I'm not sure if you have, you know? It's very important that you look after yourself."

"Well, I was just trying to get some sleep last night. You know that it doesn't make a whole lot of difference sometimes, depending on what thoughts are rolling around in your head."

"No, that's quite true," Nan agreed. "It's quite distressing really when you can't sleep, isn't it?"

"It absolutely is," Doreen muttered. She sipped the tea and smiled. "But a cup of tea is lovely, thank you."

"Well, I had to get the latest details on your love life," she explained. "We can't have people finding out these things and putting bets down."

She stared at Nan. "Please tell me that nobody's betting on my love life."

"Well, up until now," she stated in that voice that just about made Doreen cringe, "you haven't had a love life. Outside of Mack of course. And you've been pretty persistent in avoiding any kind of commitment with that poor man."

"Well, that poor man hasn't asked for a commitment yet," she stated. "And that's a good thing because I need time."

Her grandmother nodded. "And you know what? I don't think any of us realized how much time you needed. Obviously that marriage of yours was even worse than we thought."

And she had such an upset tone in her voice that Doreen reached across and gently patted her grandmother's hand. "Maybe, but it's all good."

"You mean, it's all good because you've left him," she noted.

"Yes, exactly." And then she laughed. "Besides, he's still trying to figure out how to get me to agree to less money."

"Did he call you again?" Nan asked, horrified.

Doreen nodded. "And I just hung up on him."

She cackled. "That's good. That should make your lawyer happy."

"I think so. He seems to think that, because my ex is calling me all the time, he's ready to cave in. But I don't know."

"You don't think he is?"

"He doesn't cave in easily to anything," she murmured. "But I doubt he would want to go to court over it all. He wants to settle out of court, so that he can keep his notoriety down. Nothing's more difficult in the business world than having a wife run amok."

At that, Nan nodded. "And that's why I am a little worried about you, you know?" she admitted almost apologetically. "If you've become such a liability, what are the chances that he'll do something about it?"

"I don't know. I disappeared once on him, and he didn't seem to have a problem with that."

"Sure, but you weren't taking all his money with you," she added in a dry tone.

"I'm not taking all his money now either," she declared. "I honestly don't know what Nick's been asking for, but apparently my ex has megamillions," she shared.

At that, Nan stared at her, fascinated. "And speaking of money," she added, "how'd you hook up with Bernard?"

"He's connected to this diamond case."

Nan immediately nodded. "Of course, it's his ex-fiancée's engagement ring." And then she rolled her eyes. "I mean, that girl was a child."

"Well, she was of legal age, I'm sure," Doreen noted. "But there's no doubt that she was definitely young for Bernard."

"And yet Bernard likes them young."

"That's true. I would agree with that," Doreen noted thoughtfully. "But then again I think he likes women."

"He's alive, and he's breathing, so of course he does." Nan chuckled. "Men, they're all the same."

At that, Doreen shook her head. "I don't think I can lump Mack into that same category."

"No, he's been incredibly patient with you," she agreed. "I was kind of hoping that maybe that would develop into something."

At that, she stared at her grandmother. "I'm not going there right now," she replied quietly. "I've told you that it's too early."

"And you're stuck on trying to get rid of that husband of yours first?"

"Isn't that fair?" she asked curiously. "I mean, how is it fair to Mack to offer him anything less than all of me?"

Nan stopped and stared at her granddaughter for a long moment, and then she nodded very slowly. "You know something, my dear? I love your ethics," she replied. "And you're right. Mack does deserve all of you. So now you get that darned divorce, even if you have to accept a little bit less money, and then turn your attention to Mack. He's been waiting a long time."

Chapter 20

LATER THAT AFTERNOON Doreen still pondered any motivation for why this woman, if it were Candy, had gone to that consignment store. That was the incongruency that just made no sense. Doreen knew it would make sense at one point in time, but she wasn't sure what it would take to make that kind of truth come out. What she really wanted to do was talk to Wendy's assistant, who had come in those few days to help Wendy. Doreen wondered if she had seen this woman.

Rather than phoning Wendy yet again, Doreen decided to take the animals, wander down, say hi to Esther, check out the quince tree, and once again wander up and down that alleyway, looking for the ring. It didn't make any sense that she would find the ring there, but this might help Doreen get a much better idea of what could have happened. And, with her animals in tow, she slowly walked in that direction.

As she got closer, Goliath got a little more difficult. She finally got frustrated, picked him up, and carried him. He meowed at her and batted her chin with sheathed claws. At least he wasn't mad at her, but she didn't know what was going on now that he was acting this way. But she had long ago learned that the animals knew things she didn't. When she got around the corner and came up the alleyway she stopped because there was the van.

She marched forward, carrying Goliath, Mugs racing at the end of the leash now, and Thaddeus perched on her shoulder, his streamlined beak pointed toward the men.

Almost immediately the driver hopped out and glared at her. "Now what are you doing back here again?" he asked in disgust. "Like we don't have enough problems with nosy people.'

Immediately Goliath didn't like his tone and squirmed in her arms. "Oh, somebody else doesn't like you hanging around, huh? Or are you into tormenting all the neighborhood, not just Wendy's place? Maybe you're the one going through Esther's garbage too, are you?"

He glared at her. "You don't know anything."

"Nope, sure don't, and there's absolutely nothing that you're saying that'll ever give me any more information either."

He shook his head at her. "Busybody woman, you should really learn to keep your mouth shut."

"Think so?" She laughed at that. "You know what? I'm slowly starting to understand what makes guys like you tick. And I admit that I've not exactly been the fastest learner at it, but really it's all about greed."

He stared at her, frowning. "That ring's worth a lot of money, he protested. "That's enough to set people up for life."

She nodded. "It is, indeed." And she didn't even think about mentioning the fact that it could be just the fake one they were looking for. "The question is, how did you know that Candy had it?"

At that, he stared at her, and a blank look came over his face, but it was forced, as if he'd reached up, grabbed a screen, and dropped it. "I don't know who you're talking about."

"Yeah? Well then, you haven't done your research," she said, with a laugh. "And you're bound to be very disappointed at the end of this day."

He shook his head at her. "You don't know what you're talking about," he replied. "Keep your nose outta other people's business."

Goliath responded with a low growl, which Rodney didn't seem to hear. "Well, if you'd leave Wendy alone, that'd be fine," Doreen stated. "But you seem determined to get yourself into trouble. But then—with a record like you've got—hey, that kind of trouble just comes naturally to you."

Immediately he stepped toward her, his fist clenching. Mugs started to bark and jump up at the end of his leash. "Shut the dog up," Rodney uttered in a low, angry tone. "Or I'll shut it up for you."

"Yeah, you think so? He might not look like much," she noted quietly, "but he's got quite a reputation in town."

He sneered at that. "I can kick the dog down. It's not like there's anything to him. Now if you'd had a decent-size dog," he admitted, "maybe I'd be scared, but not looking at this thing."

"Yeah? And how about the cat?"

He looked at the cat in her arms and started to laugh. "Good God." He looked over at his buddy. "You know what? This is just too funny to be real."

Mugs barked and tugged at his leash, which had Rodney backing up one step.

Then Goliath gave a huge howl, which scared Rodney away another step.

Doreen almost laughed. Instead she nodded. "I'm not sure Samuel agrees."

At the mention of his name, Samuel gasped.

But the driver, whose name was Rodney, gave her an ugly look and said, "You have a big mouth."

"Yeah, I do, *Rodney*," she replied immediately. "And you have a record and are a bully, threatening Wendy."

He shook his head. "We want what's ours."

"You mean, what you stole."

"You don't know anything about it," he snapped grimly. "And you don't know that we stole anything."

"Well, guys like you," she noted, "that's what you do."

The driver stepped gingerly toward her, testing the animals' responses. "And you're getting a little bit too mouthy for your own good," he replied, his tone low.

Mugs's barking and Goliath's howls froze him where he was.

"Yeah. See? You don't have any murders in your record yet," she shared. "A lot of car thefts and maybe some, you know, other problems in terms of not getting along with people. Of course all that comes along with the lifestyle you lead," she stated coolly. "But, if you are thinking or planning on taking that step into assault, particularly of a woman and her pets for no reason, well, you'll get a lot more jail time."

"I'm only getting jail time," he noted, with a fat smile, "if I get caught.

She nodded. "Good point. But, if you think you won't get caught, when there are cameras all around this place now, then that's a whole different story."

He looked at her, startled, and then around the area.

"You're lying." But he didn't sound convinced.

"You think so?" she muttered. "And here you're the smarter of the two, aren't you?"

"What are you talking about?" Samuel asked. "He's not smarter than I am."

At that, the driver just rolled his eyes. "Get in the van. We're leaving."

"We didn't talk to the owner yet," Samuel protested. "You said we would have a serious talk with her today."

"Yeah, well, your *serious talk* isn't happening," Doreen stated coolly. "And, if you had any brains, you'd ditch this guy and find another place to go be a jerk."

At that Samuel glared at her. "You're the one who needs a tune-up."

"Yeah?" She smiled, taunting him by saying, "let me know how that works out for you."

At that, Rodney stepped forward. "I don't know why you're so cocky." He studied her carefully.

"I've met guys like you before," she explained, with a toss of her head. "Bullies. Losers. Every one of you," she muttered. "That's all right. Keep going through life, beating up people, trying to steal things. Karma will catch up with you. I mean, getting a real job never was on your radar, was it?"

He stared at her. "It doesn't make any sense that you don't know to be scared." He looked back at the kid. "Come on. I said get in the van." He walked back to the vehicle. "We'll be back."

"I'm counting on it," she said, with a big smile. "Maybe bring Candy too next time."

He stared at her, opened the driver's side door, then shook his head and slammed it shut again and walked back toward her. "What do you know about Candy?"

"A lot more than you think I do," she noted quietly. "And how sad is that?" She shook her head at him. "You should be ashamed of yourself."

"You don't know nothing," he snapped. "You're just trying to get information out of me now."

"I don't need to. She's on the run. She took the ring. She's lost it, and so have you, and now you think that somebody, Wendy here, should pay."

He stared at her. "Well, if you know where it is, I'd be happy to listen to you."

"Yeah, that's not happening but nice try. I suppose you're after the reward, huh?"

At that, his frown deepened. "What do you know about the reward?"

"Everybody knows about the reward," she replied. "Most people don't give a crap though."

"Oh, but you're different, right?" he asked, with an eye roll.

"Well, if I heard a reward was offered, I'd probably accept it," she admitted. "Why wouldn't I? But it's not like it's offered still."

"Sure it is," Rodney confirmed. "The reward is still out there. We checked."

"Sure did." And that came from Samuel.

"I think people involved with the theft of the missing diamond are not eligible for the reward. But you might want to remember or at least to learn a whole lot more about the facts," she shared quietly. "But then I guess that's just a little bit too much for you to sort out, isn't it? I mean, if you're going by what Candy told you, that's not really something reliable."

"Hey, you calling Candy a liar?"

"I know she's Samuel's cousin," Doreen stated, with a wave of her hand.

At that revelation came a deadly silence. Rodney turned to look at Samuel. "How the hell does she know that?" he asked Samuel in a low hard tone that looked like Samuel would pay for it.

"There had to be a connection between among the pair of you, Candy, and finding the missing ring….," she explained. "I mean, had to be. And guess what? You guys are it." She chuckled. "But that is not necessarily the death sentence you seem to think it is."

"Sure it is," Rodney declared. "*Nobody* should know that." He turned to glare at Samuel again.

"Well, we all do," she repeated, with a hard tone. "So stop making it sound like Samuel's the one who's in trouble. You knew."

"Sure I knew. That doesn't change anything. *You* aren't supposed to know."

"Oh, it doesn't take much to figure out you guys."

He glared at her. "So what do you know about Candy then?"

"Not a whole lot." Yet she chuckled. "I mean, except that she's on the run. So either Joel is no longer in the picture, or you guys have another reason for pushing her into running."

At the name *Joel*, Rodney stiffened.

She nodded. "Yeah. Didn't think I knew about him either, did you?"

"You are dangerous," he muttered.

"Yeah, I sure am," she agreed quietly. "I'm also telling you to lay off of Wendy here."

"Or else what?" he asked, with a sneer.

"Well, your friends are waiting for you back in jail," she noted, unconcerned.

It was the unconcerned part that she knew was getting to these guys. And the fact of the matter was that she was very concerned, and she knew that Mack would have her head when he reviewed the street cam tapes later today, if the cameras had gone up—which was one of the reasons she'd come down to check on Wendy. Doreen didn't know if they were live after these goons had destroyed them on one of their earlier visits. The city should have repaired them already, but not everything went the way it should have. Even at that thought, she groaned at herself. "You better take off," she shared. "The cops will be here any moment."

He shook his head at her. "I'm still not sure what your game is."

"And that worries you, huh?"

He nodded. "It does. If you think you'll get that reward off me," he stated, "there's no way."

"Of course because you feel that you deserve it, right?" she stated, with a nod. "I mean, after all you've been through in life, the world owes you something, so why not the reward? Doesn't matter that Candy's trying to sell the ring or doing something with it, and that makes absolutely no sense."

"It's been a long time since Candy made any sense," he stated, with an eye roll. "That woman has gone down the drain real fast.

"And I'm sorry for her," she said. "It's not how she thought life would go."

"When you hook up with guys like Joel, life goes in directions you don't really expect."

She nodded at that. "And that's kind of what I suspected but had hoped not," she shared. "Candy was young, too young for what happened."

"And all she had to do was stick close," Rodney snapped, "but she blew that, so that's not my fault. And in no way am I losing that reward to you."

She smiled. "So I'm not sure, but is that a dare?"

He stared at her in shock. "Why are you not scared?"

"I've got a secret weapon," she shared.

Just then Goliath had had more than enough confrontation, and he jumped down, howling.

"What did you do to the cat?" Rodney asked, taking a step back.

"He's pissed at the way you're talking to me," she murmured. "Goliath here knows about social etiquette, and, if you don't behave yourself, he gets a little perturbed."

At that, the guy snorted. "You're nuts."

"Yeah, I've heard that a couple times," she agreed easily. "And, I mean, I won't tell you that you're wrong, but I will tell you that, if you want to stay out of jail for the rest of today, you better take off."

"And if I don't?"

"I don't care." She shrugged, with a bright smile. "I'm happy to talk some more. I mean, like where's Candy now?" she asked. "Is she still on the run from you guys? What did you do to her anyway?"

"She's not on the run from us," Samuel protested.

At that, Rodney turned to his partner and yelled, "Shut up. She's just gunning for information."

"And you'll give it to me," she stated cheerfully.

"Well, if you know so much, you don't need any information," Rodney argued, with a laugh.

"Yeah, but you know what? The ring is somewhere," she said. "All I have to do is find it."

At that, the back door opened, and Wendy stepped out nervously. She looked at Doreen and then the men. "Are you okay?" she asked Doreen, trying to keep her voice calm and brave.

"I'm fine." Doreen laughed. "We were just discussing Candy and her involvement in all this."

But the men were already moving back to the vehicle.

Doreen nodded. "Smart," she noted. "I told you. When the cops get here, they'll be quite pissed at you."

Rodney glared at her. "That reward is ours."

She shrugged. "You have to find the ring first," she replied. "And you're the one who dared me."

"I did not," he argued.

At that, Samuel looked at him and said, "Well, you kinda did."

Almost immediately Rodney smacked Samuel hard across the face. And then in an ugly tone he said something to him, and Rodney got into the vehicle.

She looked over at Rodney and nodded. "Now, Samuel, you know what you're dealing with. So you may want to change your friends, before you end up in deep trouble."

But Samuel was already in the vehicle and didn't say anything. Yet he looked surly and a little stunned. And she realized that this was a change in their relationship all of a sudden.

As they drove off, Doreen figured that Rodney had never lifted a hand against the kid before. Hopefully it'd be an eye-opener. It was also a warning to her. She understood the message; she just wasn't too sure what she was supposed to do about it. She'd never been all that great at listening to bullies and their idle threats.

When she heard another sound, she turned to look at the back door to Wendy's store only to find Mack standing there, glaring at her.

She groaned. "How did you know?"

"What? That you're in trouble?" he asked, his fury quietly banked. "Wendy called me."

Doreen looked at Wendy, and Wendy shrugged.

"Once I saw them there, I knew it was trouble. I didn't know you were here."

"Ah." Then she beamed at Mack. "See? You came to help Wendy, not because I was in trouble."

"I should have guessed." He motioned toward the store. "Shall we?"

She glared at him. "I'm here to walk around this back alley. And to visit with Esther."

His jaw worked. "And you want to explain what all that was just now?"

"They were threatening me," she replied. "And Wendy."

"And yet I didn't hear them," Wendy said. "What did they say?"

Doreen quickly relayed the conversation to them. "It's really the reward they're after," she noted.

At that, Wendy nodded. "I get that. I don't know why anybody would put up a reward for something like this or at least leave it still valid after ten years. It just brings in all the crazies. And I really don't know why they're looking around here."

"I'm pretty sure Candy used the excuse to sell you the ring."

At that, Wendy stopped, looked at her, and repeated, "Excuse?"

Doreen nodded. "*Excuse.* Wendy, when you put clothes outside, stuff that you're not keeping, that you'll just throw away, what do you do with them?"

"Well, it depends. I mean, the dumpster bins are right there." And she pointed.

"And does anybody else use the dumpster bins?" she asked.

"All the homeless around town go through it, I'm sure," Wendy suggested. "But I don't really worry about it. Why?" She was obviously confused.

Doreen nodded. "I'm just trying to figure out all possible scenarios."

Mack looked at her, frowning. "But you seem to think you have some kind of a working theory."

She nodded. "Now that I do, I'm not quite ready to tell you." He glared at her. She shrugged. "I get it. I get it. You want me to. But I don't think what I have will hold water yet."

"And how long do you expect that to take?" he asked, with exaggerated patience.

She thought about it and shrugged and offered, "Maybe by tomorrow?"

At that, Wendy gasped. "Seriously?" she cried out in delight. "Can you have this solved by then?"

She looked back at Mack to see him frowning at her.

"And can you do it without getting into trouble?" he asked, raising an eyebrow.

She snapped, "Well, I would like to think so."

"Yeah, I would too," he agreed. "But you do seem to have this penchant for trouble."

"I think trouble follows me," she added. "I'm not really sure how that works."

"Well, it works," he noted, with a sigh, "because you keep putting yourself in a position where trouble can find you."

She looked at him and frowned. "You know what? That kind of makes sense."

"Good. You want to stop then?" he asked quietly.

She shook her head at him, still frowning. "You know I can't." She tried to let him down gently. "I know you're worried about me, and I appreciate that."

He sighed. "But not enough to get yourself out of trouble, *huh*?"

"It's not even that," she explained, "but Wendy's life won't be improved until we fix this."

"And you can fix this?" Wendy asked in joy, clapping her hands together.

"I think so," Doreen replied. "I'm just not … I have to find the actual items first."

At that, they both stopped and looked at her. Mack asked, "Items? Plural?"

She nodded grimly. "Yes, items. And, no, I won't elaborate, at least not right now."

At that, Mack reached over, grabbed her hand, and stated, "It would be safer for you, and I sure would feel better, if you'd elaborate on some things, whether you feel like they are shored up or not."

She glared at him. "Are you sure I have to do that right now?" she asked suspiciously.

"You really don't want to tell me what you're up to?"

"I don't think you'll believe me yet," she replied, then winced. "And, no, it's not a judgment on you. It's just a sign of the times."

He stared at her. "And what times would that be?"

"The times of trouble that certain people have been in," she replied. "And I know that sounds very nefarious too, and I don't mean it to be."

He sighed. "Everything with you sounds nefarious."

But, at that, Wendy was her defender. "Let her continue, please," she said. "If she can get these guys off my back and if we don't have to have the police involved and if it doesn't become violent, that would be the best."

"It would be," Doreen agreed. "But, more than that, we would also put yet another mystery behind us."

He stared at her in wonder. "You know what? If I didn't know you, I'd say something about this being a load of crap. But because I do know you …"

She waited and then nodded. "You'll trust me, right?"

He sighed. "I'll trust you somewhat," he clarified. "What I can't have is you getting hurt."

She looked up at him mistily and said, "I promise."

But he was having none of that. "You can't promise such a thing. So many times you're the one who ends up injured. And that, we've had enough of."

"Okay, maybe I'll make sure it's somebody else this time."

He stared at her. "You'll make sure? You can't promise that either."

She shrugged. "Well, if it's not me, it must be somebody else then, right? But I don't know who yet."

"Good," he replied in defeat. "I'll give you until tonight, and then I want details."

"But that's only until tonight," she cried out. "That's not enough time."

"It'll have to be," Mack stated. "You'll just need to work faster."

QUARRY IN THE QUINCE

And, with that declaration, and a smug look, he walked back into the store. "Now come on," he said to Doreen and Wendy. "We need to get down the details about what just happened for the record."

Doreen groaned. "Fine, but you can't blame Wendy. She didn't even know I was here."

He snorted. "I know exactly who to blame, and it sure isn't Wendy."

And, with that, Doreen followed behind him.

Chapter 21

DOREEN WATCHED MACK drive away, bringing an end to all the questions that he'd had, also taking Goliath and Mugs back to the house for her. By the time she had slipped out of Wendy's store, giving her a wave, the store was full of customers again. Doreen was happy for Wendy, but, at the same time, Doreen needed to bring this missing diamond case to an end and fast, before people got really tired of her being around. Particularly Mack. She rolled her eyes at that.

This mystery had lain dormant for ten years. Why should she feel pressured now? But she did, and there was no doubt about it. She quickly walked around to the back alley yet again. As she passed the quince tree, she called out, just in case Esther was there. "Good afternoon, Esther."

After a moment of startled silence, then Esther asked, "Who is that?" in a testy voice.

"It's Doreen," she replied. "I just came for a walk and wanted to say hi."

At that, the gate opened, and Esther eyed Doreen suspiciously. "You're not back after more jelly, are you?"

Doreen chuckled. "No, but I certainly understand from

everybody else in town how much they were heartbroken when you stopped making it."

"I didn't stop making it," she stated, with a shrug. "I stopped going to the market and selling it. It became too much of a hassle. My mobility wasn't very good, and I decided I didn't need the money that bad."

"Understood," Doreen agreed, "but you realize you could get your customers to come to your house."

"But then I'd have to deal with people," she replied, "and I don't really want to do that."

It was hard for Doreen to argue because lots of time she didn't want to deal with people either. She nodded. "How have you been?"

"I'm fine," Ether replied. "Remember that part about not wanting to deal with people?" At that, Doreen burst into laughter. Even Esther smiled at her. "That smile of yours is infectious. You might as well come on in, now that you're here."

Taking that grudging welcome, Doreen stepped in through the gate and stopped when she saw the crows up on the quince again. "Did you give up trying to chase them away?"

"No, but I got my safety pin back," she replied, with a cackle.

"I hear you can tame them pretty easily," she murmured.

At that Thaddeus poked his head out and said, "Thaddeus is here. Thaddeus is here."

"Yes, Thaddeus is here," she cooed at her bird. Then turning to Esther, she asked, "And how did you get it back?"

"Banging the tree," she stated, with an eye roll. "I knew he'd stolen it. And I don't know about taming them, and I'll only say it to you, but sometimes they are good company."

Doreen looked at Thaddeus and nodded.

"That's how you feel about him, isn't it?"

"Absolutely it is," she replied gently. "Thaddeus is my friend."

At that, Thaddeus preened. "Thaddeus's friend. Thaddeus's friend."

Doreen chuckled. "Not always a good friend." And then she laughed because Thaddeus gave her a gimlet eye.

Esther grinned at their antics. "Well, if you're ever missing anything, check the tree."

At that, Doreen nodded, turning serious. "I was wondering about that. Something went missing a long time ago, and the rightful owner would really like it back."

"Well, it's probably up there," she said. "The birds love anything shiny."

"That's what I was thinking," she muttered. She looked at Thaddeus. "Hey, Thaddeus, you want to go visit?"

Thaddeus poked his head back out from underneath her hair and looked at her. She pointed up to the tree. And then she put him on a branch. "Why don't you go up there and see if something shiny is up there?"

Almost immediately, several crows surrounded Thaddeus. But instead of being scared, he preened some more. "Thaddeus's friend. Thaddeus's friend."

She wondered if she'd done the right thing, frowning now. "Maybe I'll go up with him."

At that, Esther laughed. "It's a big tree, but it's not that strong," she explained. "Plus it's old. Some of the branches have broken. But, if you want, I've got a ladder."

"Oh, I want," she exclaimed.

And, with that, Esther headed over to the side of the house, where she pointed out a ladder. Doreen grabbed it, brought it to the backyard, propped it up against the tree, and slowly climbed up, talking to Thaddeus the whole time. "How're you doing, Thaddeus? See anything up there?"

But he was hooked on visiting with his new friends, walking back and forth, with his chest out.

"Good Lord," she said, "you're just showing off."

The crows muttered among themselves but didn't seem to be too bothered by the presence of Doreen or Thaddeus. They were probably trying to figure out what this crazy bird was in their midst. But they weren't attacking him, so she was grateful. She wasn't so sure what would happen when she got a little closer to their stash. She asked Esther, "How long have they been hanging around?"

"Well, they keep breeding and coming back," she noted, "so we're probably on like the eighth or ninth or tenth generation." Esther laughed.

"And how long ago?"

"Ever since my fruit trees started having fruit."

"So you must get a lot of other birds too then?"

"Yeah, but these guys may be here more so because of the dumpsters, I would think. I don't know," she said, raising her palms. "Maybe they just like me yelling at them."

Doreen poked her head out from the branches and grinned at Esther. "You know what? I wouldn't be at all surprised. Thaddeus doesn't seem to like it when I yell at him, but he doesn't seem to be terribly bothered either."

"Exactly," Esther agreed. "It was kind of a joke with my husband. He used to come out all the time and try and chase them away, but I don't know that he tried to chase them away as much as just spend time with them. He was always a bird lover. Which is why I don't kill them very much."

"But you have killed them in the past?"

She nodded. "Sure, but usually not very many—and that was a long time ago, after my husband died."

At that, Doreen turned and looked at her. "That's an interesting reaction."

"Yeah, well, I was mad at him."

She wanted to laugh at that but didn't dare. "Mad at him for dying?"

"Darn right," she declared. "We promised to grow old together." And then she sneered. "And he broke his promise. You wait until I see him in heaven. I'll tell him what I think of that."

It was all Doreen could do to keep a straight face, but she could see that, from Esther's point of view, it was serious business, and she meant it. "You know what? I hadn't considered death that way," she noted.

"You should."

"Well, it depends that you get married of course. And I gather he didn't grow old and die."

"Died in an accident," Esther replied quietly. "And he wasn't supposed to."

"No, I don't think anybody's ever supposed to die in an accident. That's why they're called accidents."

At that, Esther snorted. "Good point," she muttered, "but I was angry at him. I didn't want to be alone getting old. It's hard getting old, but getting old *alone* is even harder," she muttered. "And, if you're not careful, you'll find that out for yourself."

"I might," Doreen agreed cheerfully. "So far, I upset more people than I make friends."

"Well, if you would stop trying to put them in jail all the time," Esther noted, with a cackle, "they might stay friends."

"Obviously you've heard about me."

"Yep, and I looked up some more after you left the other day," she said, still laughing. "But what do you expect? I mean, even people who befriended you, you turned on them."

"Well, not really," she said, turning to look at her. "I was just solving a murder."

"Yeah, but you ended up sending them away."

She winced. "I know, and now I don't make friends, and then I don't have to feel like I'm a traitor."

"Oh, now there's a thought," Esther teased, still laughing at her. "Don't make friends, and then you won't have to feel guilty when you put them behind bars."

"Yeah, that's kind of my thought process," Doreen confirmed.

"What about Mack?"

At that, she froze, slowly poked her head back out of the tree, where she was trying to climb a little higher. "What do you know about Mack?"

"I have my sources," she noted. "You have sources too, but I wonder which one of ours is better."

"Probably yours," she admitted. "I don't have years of experience living here to garner that kind of a loyal base."

"Besides, I have something to bribe them with too." Esther chuckled.

At that, Doreen called out, "Yeah, jelly. Believe me. Nan and Mack have forewarned me that all kinds of people would try to get some of that off me."

"Did you sell it?" Esther asked in an ominous tone.

"Nope, I sure didn't, but I will confess to giving Nan a jar or six. She was absolutely over the moon when she found out I had some."

"Well, that's fine. She's your grandmother. You're supposed to look after her."

"That was my thought," she replied, "but I was hoping it wouldn't make you too angry."

"Like you care," she snapped. And then she asked, "Did you find anything yet?"

"Well, I see Thaddeus, who seems to be hopping from branch to branch and going higher and higher along with the crows. I'm not sure what's going on with that."

"They're all talking and chittering back and forth," Esther explained. "You know—almost like teatime between them. Which is kind of bizarre, considering they're a very different species."

"I don't know," Doreen replied. "I think most humans are too. I mean, particularly if you've met some of them."

"Oh, you're so right," Esther agreed. "I have met some of them, all right. Some of the weirdest, wildest, wackiest people ever."

"Yeah, that's just kind of how it works," she stated. "And just when you think you're getting somewhere, you find out you're not."

"I won't argue with that either," Esther declared.

As soon as Doreen got a little bit higher, Esther called up to her. "Move to the left a bit, and there should be a big haul of stuff there. My husband used to go up there all the time to clear it out."

Hearing branches creak, Doreen shifted ever-so-slightly.

"And don't fall down," Esther snapped. "I'm not calling you an ambulance."

Rolling her eyes at that, Doreen reminded her, "I'm still on the ladder."

"Yeah, but it's pretty easy to fall," she added.

Doreen would not argue with her because Esther was

probably correct. Doreen leaned over to the side, using the branch for stability, and that's when she saw a stash. "You're not kidding about a stash. Wow, I wonder if they just inherit this from one generation to the next?"

"I think they just take it over," Esther guessed. "We had one crow about ten years back that would steal anything and everything. My husband went up there several times to get stuff."

"What kind of stuff?"

"Oh, everything from socks to watches," she stated. "I didn't even think they could carry that kind of stuff."

"Yeah? What about rings?" Doreen asked.

"There was a bunch, mostly costume jewelry." Esther shrugged. "I don't know. He left them a bunch of stuff too because he didn't want to steal everything. He took what he wanted to take, and then he left them the rest, hoping it would make them happy."

Doreen smiled at anybody leaving a crow things in their nest to make them happy, but, hey, you know what? She would probably do the same thing. As she looked in on the nest, which was more like a cardboard box that had been stuffed full, she found everything from straight pins, needles, pieces of tin foil, metal twist ties, plastic twist ties, bread clips—everything you could think about. "So how many safety pins do you want?" she asked Esther.

A gasp came from down below. "Have those little buggers stolen more?"

"Quite a bunch are here." Doreen chuckled. "So I'll say yes."

"Wow." She thought about it and said, "I need about four or five."

"Okay, hang on." And with that, she added, "Heads-up.

I'm dropping them down." And she dumped five of them overboard. She heard a scrabbling in the grass below her.

"I got four," Esther replied.

"I did send five, but maybe you can't see one."

"That's okay," Esther stated. "Four's enough. If I need more after this, I know where to come."

"Yeah, probably one dozen are still up here," she told her. "There's also some money, coins."

"You can pass that down. Money is good."

She dropped the coins that she could find and said, "There might be more in the bottom of this box. I have to keep digging." The lighting was bad here, so it was hard to see. She wondered at animals that would pick up shiny stuff like this. She was sure there was a whole psychology behind it all. And it was fascinating, no doubt, but what she was hoping to be here hadn't shown up.

As she kept digging, she saw a ring. She pulled it out and looked at it, but it wasn't the ring she was looking for. However, it was nice. "Found a nice-looking ring here too," she told Esther. "You want that?"

"Might as well toss it down," she said. "If I can get a few bucks for it, why not?" And that's what she did.

Took Doreen several more minutes to go through the stash, and, when she finally got down to the bottom, her disappointment was immeasurable. She groaned. "And here I thought for sure it would be here." She kept digging around a little bit more and then realized there was another layer, as if more twigs and branches had gone in on top to separate the two layers. She had watched birds build complete nests in one day's time, so she shouldn't be surprised.

She quickly shifted around and heard the birds starting to caw and getting angry at her being there. "Just give me a minute longer," she told them.

"They're getting quite agitated," Esther called out. "You wouldn't want to push it too much further."

"No, I know." She reached for another handful to sift through, and her hand landed on something large and hard, like a ring. She pulled it up and smiled. She quickly stuck it on her finger, and, with the crows now crying around her and swooping and diving, she stepped down on a few more rungs of the ladder and called out to Thaddeus. "Thaddeus, come on."

He cried out, "Thaddeus is here. Thaddeus is here."

But he made no attempt to jump down toward her. She frowned at that. "Come on, big guy. It's time to get you outta here. These guys aren't real happy with me."

"Thaddeus is here. Thaddeus is here."

But he still wasn't coming. She groaned. "This is not a good time for you to make your bid for independence," she stated. "Nan loves you."

At that, Thaddeus called out, "Thaddeus loves Nan. Thaddeus loves Nan."

"Well, show it, please, and come on down." And she put out her arm, so that he could swoop down. And thankfully he marched toward her and hopped onto her arm. Feeling measurably better, she slowly made her way to the bottom of the ladder. She sighed when she held up Thaddeus to give him a kiss and a cuddle. "I was afraid there, for a minute, that I wouldn't get him back."

Esther nodded. "That's always a problem with birds, but he does appear to be quite happy with you."

"Well, I hope so," she muttered. "I would be lost without him," she admitted quietly. She held out the little bit of money that she'd found on the last pass to Esther. "Here.

This was up there too. Most of their stash is tin foil and garbage bits and pieces. There's a bunch of that, which I just left up there."

"Good." Esther looked at the ring on Doreen's finger and pointed. "That's what was missing so long ago?"

"This was what I was hoping to find. Maybe it's the one from years ago," Doreen agreed, "but it could be another one just like it."

"Like fake versus real? I'm not a fancy jewelry kind of person anyway, so I couldn't tell which."

"Right," she murmured. And, with that, she grabbed the ladder and told Esther, "Let me put this back for you."

"Now," Esther stated, her hands on her hips, "I suppose you want payment for going up there and getting my safety pins, don't you?"

"Nope, sure don't," Doreen cried out cheerfully. "Just happy we got them back for you, and I had a chance to go take a look for what I was searching for too."

"You really just wanted that ring, didn't you?"

"Yep." She nodded.

"It's really ugly. You know that, right?" Esther said gently.

At that, Doreen laughed. "It *is* really ugly, but beauty is in the eye of the beholder."

Esther shrugged. "Well, it's all yours."

"Thank you, Esther."

As Doreen walked toward the rear gate, Esther called out, "Come back another time. That was fun."

And, with a laugh, Doreen smiled at her and waved. "Sure, I'll come and visit again." And she let herself out of the gate.

The usual walk home was hard to do because she wanted

to run. She wanted to take a closer look at the ring, now in better lighting, but no way she would do that while she was walking. So she kept the ring turned around on her finger, with her hand fisted around it. Even if somebody stopped to talk to her, she would make sure that it wouldn't show. She should have stuffed it in her pocket, but now she felt too conspicuous to do that in public. She had no idea if this was the original ring, the real diamond one, or even close to being Bernard's missing diamond ring. And, even if it was Bernard's, was it then the real ring or the imitation ring?

That was, of course, Doreen's next problem.

Chapter 22

LEAVING ESTHER, DOREEN turned the corner heading toward home. She wasn't too far away, if she could get there safely and just in time. As she came up to the cul-de-sac, she felt some of the relief unfurling inside her. Now to just make it inside. As soon as she got up to her front door though, Richard opened his front door and glared at her.

She smiled. "Hi, Richard," she said in an amiable tone. "Nice day, isn't it?"

"Well, it was," he groused. "Until that van came driving by, honking."

"What van?" she asked, staring at him in astonishment.

"Dunno, a big white van," he replied, and he repeated three of the letters of the license plate. "Two guys driving." He nodded. "Yeah, and it was obvious they were honking at your place."

"Yeah, they're kind of a pain," she stated carefully. "Don't talk to them if they come by, okay?"

"Why is that?" he asked suspiciously.

"Because they're criminals," she murmured.

He stared at her in horror and quickly stepped inside, slamming the door behind him. She unlocked her front door, stepped inside, closed it, and relocked it, happy to have her animals greeting her. She stopped to pet them all, then raced through the main part of the first floor of the house into the kitchen, just to make sure that nobody was here and then checked out the backyard. She also checked the second floor and confirmed the place was empty.

With that and a sense of great relief, she sat down at the kitchen table, took the ring off her finger, grabbed her magnifying glass, and took a careful look. Her hands shook when she checked it once, put it down, took several deep breaths, lifted her magnifying glass, and checked it again. She'd told Mack that she knew jewelry. But did she know enough about jewelry to tell a $10,000 fake and a very good facsimile against a multimillion-dollar genuine yellow diamond?

She picked it up again and looked at it carefully. But there was just no doubting that unmistakable glow and eerie quality to it. Although, if she didn't have her experience with big flashy gems, then maybe it would look cheap and gaudy …

What she didn't have, as she slowly raised her head, was any reason to understand why this ring was down there by Wendy's and Esther's places. If it had been the fake one, if this were the fake one, then she'd understand better. But the real one?

Trouble was, Bernard had paid big bucks to have a re-markable copy made, and she wouldn't expect anything less from Bernard, so she couldn't tell for sure which this ring was. And she didn't want to contact Bernard or Mack until she'd sorted it out. That thought uppermost on her mind, she got up, pocketed the ring, went over, and put on the coffee. As she stood here, thinking about everything that had gone on and knowing that she was still missing some of the major puzzle pieces, she wanted to scream and pull her hair out.

When the coffee was done, she poured a cup. The animals were antsy and all wanted outside. She opened up the kitchen door, and the animals all raced outside. She smiled. "Yeah, we'll stay home for the rest of the day," she said quietly. "My brain hurts from thinking too much."

An odd sound came from behind her. In her kitchen. And she froze. Turning ever-so-slowly, she looked to see a woman she'd never seen before but instinctively already knew who she was. "Hello, Candy."

Mugs raced back into the kitchen, toward Candy, barking like crazy.

Doreen reached out a hand to calm him down. "Hey, buddy. I won't say everything's okay, but stand guard."

The woman laughed. "Stand guard? That's the best you can do?"

"What do you want me to do?" Doreen asked her. "I'm looking at an intruder into my own home," she glared at her. "And why are you here?"

"And how did you know that I, … what my name was?" the woman asked, looking confused for a moment. "You did call me Candy, didn't you?"

"I sure did. And?"

The woman shook her head. "I don't—" She stopped. "I don't get it. How did you know?"

"You're the only person I haven't rousted up at the moment," she explained.

At that, the woman continued to look confused.

Doreen shrugged. "Let me just say that the list of suspects was pretty narrow."

The woman shook her head. "I don't even know how you would know my name in the first place. How is it that you know that?" And then she shook her head. "Rodney told me that something was off about you."

"Yeah? What did Samuel say?"

She blinked. "Look. I just want the damn ring."

"Yeah? And why do you want the ring?" Doreen asked.

The woman stared at her. "Sentimental value."

At that, Doreen burst out laughing. "Well, that may be a reason but a flimsy one. I mean, you blew it way back when and got yourself unengaged from Bernard."

"You don't know what he was like," she said, with a shudder. "I thought I could handle it. I mean, there was so much that I really liked."

"What do you mean? So many things *about him* that you really liked?" she asked curiously. "Or just so many things about Bernard's lifestyle to like?"

The woman sniffled. "Look. You don't know what it's like to be single and alone, where everybody else has stuff, but you don't."

Doreen looked at her with a note of amusement. "You know what? I've been on both sides of that," she noted. "I definitely know which I prefer."

"Yeah." Candy nodded, as if understanding. "*Stuff.*"

"Nope, not at all," Doreen argued. "You don't understand the price that you would end up having to pay for that *stuff,*" she explained. "When I found out that you were no longer engaged, my initial thought was, *Good for you.*"

The woman shook her head. "No, you don't understand. It's not a case of *good for me* at all. If I'd been any smarter, I would have found a way to get him back again."

"He's still single," she shared. "You could always try

again. However, Bernard can't trust you now."

"No, not possible. I would try with a different rich guy."

"Towns are full of them," she said, with a laugh.

Candy looked at her. "Yeah, but they don't come after girls like me."

"They did originally," Doreen noted quietly. "I don't know what happened between the two of you, but I can guess."

She sneered. "Yeah, you and everybody else. Everybody's got something to say. Everybody tells me how I blew it. Everybody tells me how I could have done way better."

"It doesn't matter what *everybody* says," Doreen stated. "It's your life. You get to live it the way you want. I'm sorry you're not happy with the choices you made."

"And sometimes we don't really get a whole lot of choices," she muttered. "The ring, hand it over."

"And why would I do that?" she asked.

"I mean, if you think about it, it's *my* ring."

"No, it's not," she snapped.

"What do you mean? It's my ring, and, if I don't give it back, I'm in trouble."

A note of desperation was in Candy's voice. At that, Doreen stopped and stared. "Give it back to whom? I am confused."

The woman shook her head. "Good. It's not for you to figure out. This is my problem, not yours."

"Well, you're in my house, and I don't even know how you got in. I locked the door."

"I have learned a few things since I was engaged to that man."

"That man has a name," she stated, studying her.

"Yes, but it's easier for me if I say *that man*."

"Did he ever hurt you?" she asked.

"No, not like that, but I don't think he appreciated me."

Doreen wanted to smile at that. "You know what? I'm pretty sure he didn't because I'm not sure at your age anybody really understands what goes into a relationship and how to keep it going," she stated.

"Oh, and I suppose you're some sort of an expert?" Candy snapped, with an eye roll.

"Me? No, sure not," Doreen admitted. "I'm getting a divorce, and the sooner, the better, as far as I'm concerned."

"So then just give me the damn ring," she demanded.

"I don't think so. It's not yours. You don't have any right to it. And how do you know I even have it?"

She shrugged. And then she told her, "The guys set up a camera in the alley."

"A camera. Interesting."

"I think they finally figured out that you wouldn't be scared away. So they decided no more threats and to go high-tech."

"Yeah, ya think?" She smiled. "They aren't the smartest in this toy box."

"No, they aren't, but they are mean."

At that, Doreen stopped, looked at her, and asked, "Are you seriously in trouble?"

Candy nodded. "Yes."

"Right, you'll have to explain it a whole lot more for me to get that cleared up."

"I don't have to explain anything to you," she snapped.

"You do, if you want the ring. I mean, I won't just hand it over."

"Why not?" she asked almost desperately.

"Why would I? I mean, absolutely what purpose would

there be for me to give it to you? I could keep it and get the reward."

At that, Candy opened her eyes wide. "There's a reward?"

Doreen stared at her. "Well, there is for the original diamond ring." And Doreen watched as the relief crossed Candy's face. "But then, that's not the one you're after, is it?"

She shook her head. "No, I'm after the fake."

"Did you know it was a copy?"

"He told me at the time, but he also told me that I was wearing the original," she stated bitterly.

"And then, when you found out it wasn't the original, what? You felt cheated?"

"Well, what kind of really rich guy makes his fiancée wear a fake ring?" she cried out.

"Do you have any idea how many rich guys do just that?" Doreen asked her. "I mean, sure a lot of money is involved in these things, but what happens if you lose it down a kitchen sink or if you go swimming and you accidentally forget about it and you lose it? I mean, all kinds of things can happen."

"But he had it insured," she added.

At that, Doreen smiled at her. "And that's what you were counting on. Stealing the real one to get the reward, right? Maybe have the insurance company come after Bernard to get the insurance payout back?"

The woman nodded. "Yes, that is exactly what I was counting on."

"But?"

"What do you mean, *but?*" she asked. "I had the fake. I needed the real one."

"So you tried to swap them? What? A sleight-of-hand trick?"

"He didn't tell me right off the bat," she stated, with a desperate note. "And I was supposed to get the real one. It's worth a lot of money, but I didn't know how to handle it. So …"

"Of course not." Doreen nodded. "So what are you trying to do? Give the fake one to Rodney?"

Candy stared at her. "Do you know how scary he is?" she asked, her voice trembling.

"Yep, I do, but doesn't he want the real diamond?" When Candy clammed up, Doreen continued. "Do you really think that, once he takes the ring to the appraisers, he won't find out it's the fake one?"

"But it's still a really good fake. I didn't tell him that this ring was real. I told him that it was worth ten grand. And he wants it, and I need the money."

"Oh, my God, Candy. Rodney wants the real diamond. And I think you've led him to believe that you have the real one. And I think you are in a world of hurt if you hand over a fake to him. Why would he settle for the fake?"

Candy just stared at Doreen. "He gives me the ten thousand for it, and he can sell it again and get his money back. That is a lot of money."

Doreen shook her head. Maybe it was her jaded attitude rearing up, she didn't know, but it sure seemed like $10,000 wasn't worth ruining one life for, much less several lives. "I get that, in your mind, it's probably worth all that and more," Doreen began, "but it is a little worrisome that you have so little regard for the real-life way this will all come down. You know, if Rodney gives you ten thousand dollars, then he'll want something for it."

She laughed. "Of course. He wants the ring."

"And why would he expect you to hand it over to him?" Doreen asked shrewdly, knowing that there was more to this.

The woman flushed.

"He has something on you, otherwise you wouldn't be falling for this."

"Falling for what?" she asked. "You don't know anything."

"Maybe not," she admitted, "but I'm starting to get a really good understanding of people."

"He's just got something on me," she said.

"And something you're terrified that he'll use against you."

She shrugged. "Maybe."

"And has it got something to do with Joel?"

The woman stared at her. "How do you know so much?" she cried out in shock.

"And are you trying to protect Joel?"

She blanched at that. "No, you can't know that. You just can't."

"And why not?" Doreen asked, studying Candy. "I know I'm still missing something here, and that really is starting to piss me off because it shouldn't be this complicated—but you guys have made it stupid complicated."

"It's not complicated at all," she snapped. "The reason is really simple."

"Of course it is." Doreen nodded. She understood now, giving a heavy sigh. "Love."

At that, Candy stared at her and started to visibly shake. "Rodney said you were strange. Are you a psychic?" she asked in a whisper.

"No, sure not," Doreen murmured. "If I were, I would

have had an easier time sorting through all this garbage." She shook her head. "And it makes me really angry that, so far, I haven't figured it out."

Of course she wasn't really angry, more like feeling foolish. Doreen wasn't any dumb bunny, and yet, right now, something was going on that she still couldn't quite understand. "Let me get this straight. You were engaged, and you decided to ditch your wealthy fiancé for a broke criminal and got Joel involved in order to get the real ring out of the safe. He did, replacing it with the fake one that you'd been wearing, but somehow you still ended up with the fake ring on your finger, *and* the real diamond ring was gone too. How did you lose both rings?"

She nodded. "We didn't know what happened either. Joel blamed me, and, well, I did wonder if he just stole the real diamond and left the safe empty. No way for me to know."

"Well, there are definitely some ways to figure this out," Doreen murmured. "From what I know, you had a big fight with Bernard, at your engagement party no less, all in front of a crowd of people. You thought you now wore the real diamond—because Joel had broken into the safe to exchange the rings, and he gave you one to wear. Was he like waitstaff or something at this party? Anyway, you staged a fight with Bernard—or had a real one, whatever—and threw away the ring somewhere, went off in a teary huff, and the whole place had a great deal of amusement at your expense, and then suddenly Bernard can't find the ring you threw away, and the one in the safe is the fake one."

Candy stared at her. "That's not bad," she said in a teary tone. "You're still missing a bit, but that's … that's not bad."

"Of course I'm missing a bit," she snapped. "Because

something's still wrong with this. But, if we're closer on this now, … what happened with you when you gave Joel the fake one?"

"He was really angry at me, blamed me, said that I was too stupid to know what a real diamond was from a fake one," she replied, wiping back tears.

"Well, these are very expensive fakes," Doreen noted. "So I can't say that I'm terribly surprised."

"I told him that, but he didn't believe me. He blamed me, said that I'd done it on purpose and that I was trying to take the money for myself."

Doreen looked at her. "And were you?"

"Of course not," she snapped. "It's only been him for me."

"But did Joel believe you though?" Doreen asked. "Because you know these guys. Whether Bernard, Joel, Samuel, or Rodney, once they get something in their heads, they're not really reasonable after that."

"No, they aren't," she agreed. "And Joel told me that I had to get the fake back, if nothing else."

"I still don't understand this fixation on having the fake ring. Plus it's been ten years since the real diamond went missing, which means you had the fake for the past decade. So why now? Why does Joel want the fake now? That's another part I don't understand."

She shuddered. "Joel's been in jail. The whole time he's been in jail, I thought it was over and done with."

"And what did he get picked up for?"

"It was nothing to do with that ring," she cried out, making the mistake of looking at Doreen. "Okay, it kind of had to do with the ring. He'd stolen a car, and we were running away to Vancouver. He stopped to get the ring appraised there. Found out it was the fake. He was so angry when we left there. He finally pulled the car over on the side of the road. Now he was really yelling at me, hitting me. Somebody must've called the cops. And Joel has a record, so, when the cops found out who he was and ID'd the vehicle as stolen, the cops arrested him on the spot. And he remained in jail until he saw a judge, who gave him a hard sentence as a repeat offender. Joel thought he'd get away with a light sentence. Then, back in jail, he got into some fights, and, well, that sentence just kept growing."

"And so now that he's out, what?"

"He needs a new start," she said desperately. "He needs a chance to start fresh, and he needs money for that."

"So he came to you again."

She nodded, tears in her eyes. "But I had finally grown past him, only he won't let me."

"Of course not, you've been there for him the whole time, haven't you?"

"Sure," she whispered. "But I've gone to counseling, and I've done all kinds of things to sort this out and to separate myself from Joel."

"And so what is all this really about? If, even if, you do find the fake one," Doreen asked, "how does that help you?"

"Because Joel will leave me alone," she replied.

"And you really believe that?" It's obvious that Candy wanted to believe it, but she was also scared. Doreen nodded. "See? That's the thing about blackmail. Once you start paying, it never stops."

"You don't understand," she wailed. "The blackmailer is Rodney. Joel's insisting I give the real one to Rodney."

"So now Joel wants you to produce both the fake ring and the real one?" Doreen shook her head. "But you don't have either one now, right?"

"Something like that," she murmured, all the stuffing out of her by now. "I don't know anymore. Rodney believes I have the real one, but I know it's the fake. Both Bernard and the appraiser said so. Joel believes I have the fake one, and he wants the real one, which disappeared ten years ago. And I just want them all to go away."

At that, Doreen chuckled. "You know something? They're kind of close to the truth of it all."

"What do you mean?"

Doreen sighed. "Well, in order to sort it out, I'd have to bring Bernard into this. There's something that I have wondered about."

"What do you mean?"

She shook her head. "If you're up for visitors, I'll call some people to help us get to the bottom of this." And she immediately dialed Mack and luckily got him in person. "I need you here," she said loudly and clearly and then hung up. Then she phoned Bernard, even while Candy stood and stared at her. Doreen's luck held out, and she got to speak directly to Bernard. "You need to come to my house *now*." And, with that, she hung up.

Candy stared at her. "What are you doing? Don't you know how much trouble I'll be in?"

"When we get to the bottom of this, will you still be in trouble?"

She nodded. "Yeah, Rodney won't let me off the hook, and neither will Joel."

"Joel could end up back in jail anytime now," Doreen stated.

"Yeah, *could* is not the same thing as ending up in jail," Candy snapped. "And I would like to see him back in jail."

"You have anything on him?" Doreen asked.

"Sure." Candy shrugged. "I know all kinds of stuff he doesn't want me to know."

"Well, maybe then *you* can put Joel back in jail—if you have something for the police."

"What are you talking about?" she asked Doreen.

"Think about it. You're part of the reason why the real diamond ring went missing in the first place."

The woman swallowed hard. "I know, and I felt terrible about it."

"Not quite as terrible as you're likely to feel by the time this is all over with," Doreen stated. "Think about it. You were part of the attempt to steal the original."

She nodded. "I know. And I don't want to go to jail for that."

"A lot of money is riding on this right now," Doreen said.

"Bernard got insurance for it," she repeated eagerly. "So he shouldn't care."

She stared at her. "You think the insurance company doesn't care?"

She looked at her blindly. "Well, they don't though, do they?"

"You think they just pay out that kind of money and walk away?"

She nodded slowly.

Doreen shook her head. "They don't. Insurance companies get really pissy when you do insurance scams."

"Yeah, but that wasn't us."

"No, as far as I know, it wasn't Bernard either. Bernard acted in good faith, reporting his property as stolen, and, sure, Bernard did get his money's worth back, as well as he also got a broken engagement and found out that his fiancée was cheating on him."

She swallowed at that. "I didn't realize what Joel was doing in my life."

"And how about now?"

She nodded. "I've been in counseling for quite a while, all the time that I was in hiding, but he still found me."

"And so now, you're supposedly trying to lead a life on the straight and narrow, and he won't let you?"

"I was never the criminal," she stated firmly.

"Sounds like you need more counseling."

"What do you mean?" she asked.

"Being part of an attempt to steal millions of dollars in diamonds means that you were part of that criminal element."

Candy nodded. "Fine," she huffed, "but that was back then."

"Back then is still today," she muttered. "And you're just making it even more confusing." Almost immediately Doreen heard the sound of a vehicle driving up. She looked over at Candy. "So the question is, is that your friends or mine?"

She stared at her and said, "They'd better be yours because, if they are mine, we're in trouble."

Doreen watched as Candy blanched and stared nervously at the door. "You're really scared of Joel, aren't you?"

Candy nodded. "He's changed. Jail was not good for him."

"Jail generally isn't good for anybody," Doreen agreed quietly. "And, yeah, they do change in there."

Candy shook her head. "But he'd been in lots before, so I wasn't expecting it this time."

"Well, this time apparently something got a whole lot uglier."

She nodded. "And he didn't want to be there in the first place. And, when he realized he would have to stay, he got really upset."

"That's his fault, isn't it?"

Candy looked at Doreen with wide eyes. "You don't understand. Joel doesn't care whose fault it is. If he's mad, we all pay."

"Ah, one of those guys," Doreen noted, with a heavy sigh.

"Was your husband like that?"

"Absolutely," she said, with a small smile. "And you need to get clear of this guy."

"I was trying to," she snapped bitterly. "But he found me, and I don't even know how. And he wants the fake."

"And Rodney wants the real ring."

"Yes."

"*Right*," Doreen murmured.

When a second vehicle pulled up, Candy raised her eyebrows. "Things could get interesting."

"Why?" Doreen asked.

"Because …" She hesitated. "If you called for the cops, Joel won't be easy."

"Easy to take in?"

"Right."

"Has he done any crimes since he's been let out of prison this time?"

"No, he hasn't, but Rodney has." She nodded. "Rodney wants to break bones for a living," she said bitterly. "He's got that mind-set."

"Yeah, I've met him," Doreen said quietly. "He's a pretty scary dude, but I see him mostly as a bully making threats. You gotta stand up to them. We can't let guys like that run their mouths, without speaking up for yourself."

Candy just stared at Doreen. "How can you be so confident up against these guys? I mean, they're really not nice people."

"Nope, they sure aren't," she agreed quietly. "At the same time, I'm a little tired of having my life run by people like that, like my ex, so being scared is really not an issue for me. Besides," she added, "I know somebody who's on my side."

"Yeah, but they're only on your side for a little while, and then they're on their own side."

Doreen stared at Candy, who had already learned some pretty hard lessons in life. "You need to get better friends, maybe continue with more counseling. And consider reconnecting with your sister."

"No, I can't do that."

"Why not?"

"She hates me."

"I don't think so," Doreen said gently. "I talked to her recently, trying to find you."

Candy frowned, shaking her head. "I don't get why you're even involved."

"No, I'm sure you don't," Doreen replied. And then she looked over to see Mack walking into her kitchen, glaring at her, seated at her kitchen table, calmly talking to this other woman.

He asked, "What if I had been at a crime scene? I can't just be at your beck and call."

"Well, you could be at a crime scene here too, if you just give it a few more minutes," she replied. She pointed at the woman sitting nearby. "Meet Candy."

Chapter 23

M ACK HEARD THE doorbell ring not very long afterward. He walked to Doreen's front door and let in
the stranger, Mack's expression still a thundercloud.

"Mack, I presume."

He nodded and studied the stranger. "Bernard? I see
Doreen's up to her games again."

"I don't know about games," Bernard admitted, "but she
made it sound like she was in trouble."

She called out to him. "Come into the back, please, Bernard." She stood now and watched as the two men walked
into her kitchen. She smiled at Bernard. "Somebody else is
here."

He turned, looked around Doreen, and reared back.
"Candy?"

She nodded, tears coming to her eyes. She turned to
Doreen and asked in a hoarse whisper, "Why did you tell
them to come?"

"Because I think we need to know exactly what's going
on," she explained, "and the only way to do that is to have
you tell your story."

"That won't help," Candy wailed, crying out in confusion. "They'll still get really mad at me."

"These guys won't get mad at you. Too much time and effort has gone into this investigation. And, as far as Joel and Rodney go, well, they need to be stopped regardless."

Doreen looked over at Mack. "The short and simple of it is, and Candy will give us the details, Joel was in jail for the last ten years. He was in on the original heist to exchange the rings," she said, with a nod to Bernard. "Joel was to give her the real one, not the fake one, and then, Bernard, during your fight with Candy, she would disappear with the real diamond ring.

"However, they ended up with the fake ring after all, and even that got lost somewhere along the line," she added, with an eye roll. "Rodney and Candy both have some dirt on Joel, which will put Joel away for a very long time. Besides that, Rodney wants the real ring. Yet somehow he figures the fake one is the real one." She shook her head at that. "And, yes, it's confusing. And the story gets more confusing. I get that, but Rodney is no rocket scientist—nor a certified gemologist." She looked at Mack and Bernard. "So I just ask that you two listen to Candy and keep your minds open. Don't question anything yet. Can you just listen to Candy?"

Both men shared a look and then nodded.

Then Doreen turned to Candy and asked her, "Now, you want to fill them in?"

She stared at her in disgust. "What's the point? Now I'll just go to jail."

"It depends if you help Mack or Bernard or neither of them," she noted quietly. "You helping the cops keeps you out of jail hopefully. You helping the insurance company to recover a stolen gem gets them their payout monies back. And Bernard gets his expensive diamond ring back, which means a lot to him. Now you've told me that you've been in therapy for the last many years, that you want nothing to do with Joel, so this is your chance to tell us whether or not you spoke the truth."

Candy looked at her in surprise. "You really are trying to help, aren't you?"

"Yeah, I have a problem with that," she teased, sighing. "Just ask Mack here."

Mack groaned. "Yeah, that would definitely be her."

Candy looked hopefully at the two men. "She's essentially right. Ten years ago we did try to do a switch. I'm really sorry." She faced Bernard. "And, yes, when you found out Joel was still in my life, I had to make a choice, and I—unfortunately at the time—chose him." Candy wiped away more tears. "I was young and stupid."

Bernard nodded, with a clipped movement. "Yeah, you're not kidding. Go on."

Candy bowed her head. Then she looked up at Bernard and made her confession. "Joel was one of the waitstaff at our engagement party that day. He broke into your safe that day and exchanged the rings. Shortly thereafter you and I had our big argument in your house during our engagement party and broke off our engagement in front of many witnesses. I flung the ring off my finger before leaving, to throw suspicion off me.

"However, I knew the layout inside and the thick carpet at the entrance to your house, so I ended up trick throwing the ring behind me and grabbed it on the way out, when I made it look like I was fixing the strap on my shoe before tearing out of the house," she explained.

"And when Joel and I got away, we thought we had it made. For all of a few hours. We did the five-hour drive to

Vancouver in record time and went straight to get the ring appraised—and found out that it was fake. So I had worn the real one and not the fake one," she said, shaking her head. "Joel exchanged the rings for nothing. And that started the problems with Joel and me. ... He thought I was too stupid to tell a real diamond from a fake one, and I guess he was right because I couldn't tell them apart."

"Neither could Joel," Doreen added.

Candy frowned but perked up. "Right. Right. Joel didn't know either." Candy shook her head, as if shaking away some thoughts that she had been wrong about. "Then we had a rip-roaring fight on the side of the road, and the cops came by, realized the car was stolen, and arrested him on the spot. He's been in jail for the last decade, until a few weeks ago."

Mack's lips twitched. "And how did you get the combination to the safe?"

"I was seeing Joel the whole time I was seeing Bernard." She glanced at Bernard and again said, "I'm sorry."

Bernard glared at her. "I don't want your worthless apologies. I want the rest of this story."

Candy nodded, as she swallowed back tears. "I snuck Joel into the house weeks prior to our engagement party. He mounted a tiny camera, so when you opened the safe, we would hear and see the tumblers in action. I don't know how it works, but he got into the safe after that—at the party. He didn't dare take any of the money because he didn't want it to look like that we'd been in here," she added.

"And that's ... that's what happened. And then he got out of jail just recently, and he wanted the fake diamond this time, so that he could make a new start," she explained. "I have been ignoring him, hiding away, not wanting anything to do with him, to have my own new start. Somehow Joel found me, which freaked me out. And all this time he spent in jail has made him really angry about everything that got him arrested and whatever other things happened in jail. So I've been trying to get better, while Joel's gone from bad to worse."

The muscles in Bernard's cheeks twitched at that news. But he just nodded. "Abusers tend to be abusers for life," he noted quietly.

She nodded. "Very true." And she looked over at Doreen. "And now of course you want to know about how this involves the secondhand store, Wendy's place."

"Yes." Doreen nodded. "You've been working there a few days a week for the last however many weeks since Joel got out. That was a desperate move, working in Kelowna, with Bernard still living here. That makes no sense."

She stared at Doreen. "How did you know that was me?"

"Because it had to be you, looking to sell the fake ring, because you are on a short list of people who could have the fake diamond," she stated quietly. "I still don't understand why you chose Wendy to buy your fake ring instead of some pawn shop."

"Joel found me, called me several weeks ago, demanding I get money ready for him upon his release a few weeks later. I had the fake ring and other things that Bernard bought for me stashed in a storage unit here." She glanced at Bernard. "I was afraid you would have emptied the unit or changed the locks by now."

"I … Wow. I completely forgot about that." He turned to Doreen. "I'm sorry. I own units everywhere, not just here in Kelowna. The rentals are good as gold, recurring. Yet not my biggest monthly draws, so I didn't even think of that. And I do keep a few set aside for special uses, like for … this." He extended a hand, palm up, to Doreen, adding, "I would have told you, if it was even on my radar."

Doreen nodded. "I understand." Then she turned to Candy. "So I presume you raided your storage unit and took clothes recently to Wendy's, to sell on consignment."

Candy nodded. "I came back on the bus. So I asked Samuel's sister to take me to the unit, and we loaded up everything to make the trip to Wendy's. Oh my. That must have triggered Rodney as to my whereabouts. When I tried to explain to Joel that I was waiting on checks that wouldn't come until later, he went ballistic, wanted me to sell the fake ring. Luckily I did have that much. During our next call, he had the wild theory that the real diamond ring was in the pockets of the clothes I just gave away."

She sniffled. "You don't know what it's like when you have been reduced to sell clothing."

Doreen winced. "Yeah, you might want to hold judgment on that."

Candy looked at Doreen distractedly, who was sharing a look with Mack. "You don't know what Joel's like," she exclaimed. "He'll beat me up if I don't do everything he says."

Doreen raised her hand. "My ex beat me up too. So don't tell me that you have to just put up with his abuse. You stand up to these losers, these bullies."

"You just had one abuser!" Candy yelled. "I had Rodney too."

Doreen nodded. "Maybe if you would yell at them, like you are yelling at me now, it would have made a difference."

Candy closed her eyes, took several deep breaths. "I took

the fancy clothes to Wendy's consignment shop and found out how the system worked, which meant it could be months before I got a check for any clothes sold. So, right then and there, I asked Wendy for a job. And she gave me part-time work. And I got another part-time job at a diner nearby.

"I was supposed to call Joel weekly. So, on one of those calls, he decides the real diamond is in my clothes, some of which had sold already because Wendy had told me so, but some would still be there in the store. I hadn't been working there all that long, but I searched through those pieces still there. It's been ten years, and I didn't make an inventory of all those items, but I couldn't tell Joel that.

"If nothing else, I figured I could get close enough to Wendy to find out if she had ever found surprises in the pockets of the clothing she took in." Candy looked down at her hands in her lap. "Wendy never found anything but lint in the pockets and purses." She looked at the others defiantly. "I was desperate."

"And that's why you were disguised when you came in, asking Wendy if she'd buy the ring?" Doreen asked Candy.

She nodded. "I was afraid she'd recognize me. And I was pretty sure what the answer would be, but I had come to know her somewhat and figured I could tell if she was lying. If she was, then I could at least tell Joel that."

"Of course," Doreen noted quietly. "But Wendy didn't lie, and nobody's seen the original diamond ring in a decade."

"Exactly."

"And when you first came to the shop and brought all the fancy clothing to Wendy, did you go out the front door or the back door?"

Candy shook her head. "The back door. It's really humiliating having to sell your clothing."

Doreen stared at Candy and nodded. "You know what's even more humiliating?"

"What?" she asked.

"Starving. You learn a lot about what's important. When it comes down to the wire, and you have to decide whether you want food or not, then you willingly sell your clothing and choose to be embarrassed, so that you have food to live another day," she stated. "So I wouldn't be too worried about being humiliated."

Candy shrugged, waving her hand dismissively. "Whatever. I went out the back door."

"And Wendy got back to you when she sold stuff, right?"

"Exactly. Why?"

"Yeah, if you ever had the real diamond ring in a pocket of your clothing, which is a big if, chances are you may have dropped that ring in the storage unit or along the way to the storage unit, in whatever car you drove back then. Ten long years ago. Or the ring could possibly have been in one of those boxes you transported the clothes in."

Candy thought about it and nodded. "It's all possible but not very likely, yet I figured, even so, Wendy would have found it."

"No, not Wendy," Doreen clarified. "Somebody who likes to case the joint." She looked over at Mack and laughed. "You know something? Our quarry of sorts really was in the quince." She looked back at Candy. "Ten years ago, the Vancouver appraiser who looked at the ring and told you it was a fake, did he offer to buy it?"

She nodded. "Yeah, he told us that it was a decent fake,

but it was still a fake, and he'd give us maybe one thousand dollars."

"But you didn't feel tempted to do that."

"No, and Joel was too mad, and he just threw it at me. He was picked up later that same day by the cops, and meanwhile, I was busy trying to find a way to salvage my life—and to run away from Joel."

Doreen nodded and looked over at Bernard, the corner of her lips twitching. "Have you figured it out?"

He let out his breath. "All but who would have been casing the joint at Wendy's. I don't get that part."

She looked over at Mack. "What about you?"

He cleared his throat. "Cut the theatrics. I am on the clock."

"Yep, you are."

Mack got the hint that he was on the job here. He turned his glare to Bernard. "And then there's the part that you didn't ever tell anybody."

"And what's that?" Bernard asked.

"About the ring in the safe being fake."

"I told my insurance company. And the insurance company knew I had a genuine yellow diamond ring and a fake copy of the original," he admitted. "But, as it was the fake one that I was left with, it didn't matter. Not to me. Not to my insurance company."

"I don't understand," Candy cried out, staring at Bernard. "You told me that I was wearing the fake one."

"Yes, but remember? We were having an *engagement* dinner party, and, in my foolishness, I thought you should wear the real one for such a party. And I told you to give it to me that day, and I'd clean it before the party, when all I did was switch it out for the real one, figuring I'd get it back at the end of the evening," he explained. "And all hell broke loose. Only afterward did I realize that you'd gone off with the real one. I had the fake one in the safe. When I realized that you were gone, and the original ring was effectively stolen, I put in a claim."

Bernard shrugged. "It's not like the insurance company cared. Believe me. Those payouts are calculated into everybody's monthly insurance premium. So I told them all that happened, but, for a piece that expensive, you can bet my premiums went way up too. They tried to find you to get the ring back. But they never could locate you, Candy. The police report remains an open burglary case. With you as the prime suspect."

Candy blanched. "I didn't even know about that, but I guess I should have."

"Yeah, you should have," Bernard snapped. "If you had taken off with the fake one, it wouldn't have been such a problem."

Doreen now cleared her throat. "Except that would mean you seem to have two fakes now, Bernard. Your fake and Candy's fake."

By now, everyone in the room frowned at Doreen.

Bernard spoke first. "What is going on here, Doreen?"

At that Doreen stopped and smiled and asked Bernard, "Is there still a reward for the return of the original?"

"Yeah, I had a reward up from that very day, for ten thousand dollars. And I haven't pulled it down. I guess I should, considering the nefarious characters trying to get it now for their own greedy purposes."

She pulled the ring out of her pocket and held it up in her palm and said, "Or you could leave it up and give it to me."

He stared at the ring, stared at her, and picked her up and twirled her around, before putting her back down and giving her a whopper of a kiss. "Oh my God." He stared at the ring, still in Doreen's hand. Then he looked at her and asked, "But is it the real one or is it the fake one?"

At that, she laughed. "Well, you should know because you've got the fake one still, don't you?"

He nodded slowly. "I sure do. I keep it as a reminder of a harsh lesson learned, in case I ever want to be stupid and fall in love with somebody who doesn't deserve it yet again." And he glared at Candy.

Candy flushed, as she stared at the ring in Doreen's hand. "You did have it," she cried in shock. "Where? How?"

"Yep, I did," Doreen confirmed.

"And you'll hand it over now too," a man said from Doreen's rear kitchen door.

She sighed, turned to Mack, and pointed. "See, Mack? You should be happy. This time I brought you in to handle this kind of stuff." And she gave the diamond to Bernard.

Chapter 24

STARTLED, MACK LOOKED at her and then at the rear kitchen doorway, where the intruders came through, leaving it wide open in their wake. "What's this?"

Doreen looked at him and looked at the three men crowding into her kitchen, two of them brandishing guns.

"Meet Samuel, Rodney, and Joel," she said, with a sigh. "Joel, you get to head right back to prison because that's a weapon you're holding. Rodney, well, you were getting there anyway. Samuel, you're just an idiot to still be hanging around these criminals. And you should go to jail for knocking over Esther's garbage cans all the time."

Mack looked at her. "Seriously?"

She shrugged. "Be thankful I brought you here."

Samuel stared at her, like she'd grown three heads. "How did you know?"

"It's a stupid stunt. Something someone who is bored and has no life would do for entertainment."

Bernard looked at the three men and glared. "No way you're getting this ring. I went through all kinds of hell to get it."

"Yeah, *sure* you did. Sounds like my girlfriend did that,

however," Joel snapped. "Now hand it over."

Doreen looked over at Bernard. "You might want to."

He shook his head. "No, I really don't want to. I'm tired of having these people yank my chain and take what's not theirs."

"It was my girlfriend's ring," Joel spat.

"Yeah, well, we already went over that, Joel," Mack stated. "She doesn't get it. You're both lying cheating criminals."

At that, Candy added, "No, I don't deserve it, Joel. I didn't go into the engagement properly. I was a fool for trying to steal it."

Joel looked at her in disgust. "You don't even know when to keep your mouth shut, do you? God, when did you get to be so stupid?"

She stiffened and glared at him.

Doreen turned and told Joel, "You know what? You should just keep your mouth closed, before a whole pile more years get tacked on to your prison time."

"For what?" he yelled. "It's greedy busybody gold diggers like you who give us a bad name."

She raised her eyebrows. "Like me, huh?" She laughed in Joel's face, earning a hot glare coming from Mack. "Maybe, but I can tell you that busybodies, *like me*, solve these kind of problems." She looked over at Mugs. "Remember Rodney, Mugs?"

Mugs was already growling but barely a sound came out. His gaze was narrowed as he stared at the intruders.

"I told you before. If that dog comes up to me, I'll shoot it," Rodney repeated. "And where's that damn cat? I owe him a kick or two."

"Yeah, I wouldn't try that," Doreen stated.

As it was, Samuel, the only unarmed guy of the trio,

stepped up and, without a warning, decked Bernard in the face, sending him to the floor, where his hand opened, and the jewel dropped. And then a mad scramble ensued, as everybody dove for it.

Then it got even worse, between Mugs and Goliath attacking the gunmen, plus Doreen with a fry pan, while Candy screamed at the top of her lungs, and both Bernard and Mack tried to grab the guns from the two gunmen, sending wild shots into the floor. Mack got the gun away from one of them, and Doreen spied it fall to the floor, which she grabbed and fired three times out the kitchen door … into the dirt.

When everybody stopped and stared at her, she roared, "Stop. This is my house, and that's enough of this madness."

Mack had one of the gunmen in his arms, and he dropped him, giving his head an extra *thunk* against the floor, and then smiled at her. "Now I'll stop it," he said agreeably.

Bernard gave a shout of laughter and repeated Mack's motions with the gunman he was hanging on to, then handed the gun to Mack. And, with the two of the three intruders unarmed, down on the ground, and knocked out, Doreen looked for the third one, finding Samuel still standing.

She smiled at him. "Really not smart to get involved with these guys, but Mack here will take care of you."

He glared at her. "What happened to that ring?" he asked.

At that reminder, Bernard turned around, checked the two unconscious men, and started searching the kitchen. "Where is it?" he roared. "Nobody move. That ring's got to be here somewhere."

Then came a weird cackling and cawing. Everyone spun at the odd sound.

Up on top of the fridge was Thaddeus, making those weird sounds, but, in his beak, he held a bright yellow diamond ring.

"Looks like Thaddeus found it." Doreen chuckled. "But it'll cost you, Bernard."

He looked at her in surprise. "Seriously?"

She walked over to the cupboard, handed him the treat container, and said, "Yeah, really. You must pay the piper."

And he grabbed a treat and held it out to Thaddeus, who immediately dropped the ring and snatched up the treat and said, "Treat for the big guy. Treat for the big guy."

And the place burst out in laughter.

Well, … except none came from Samuel, Rodney, Joel, and Candy.

Bernard spoke up. "So tell me the rest of the story, Doreen. Before these buffoons interrupted."

Doreen laughed. "Between Mack and an honest appraiser, you should be able to confirm my theory. I presume the Vancouver appraiser was dishonest in his appraisal of Candy's supposed fake diamond ring. He was offering to pay a thousand dollars for a multimillion-dollar ring, thinking to pull a fast one over on Candy and Joel, who were just passing through and who didn't know fine jewelry.

"So Candy had the original diamond ring all this time, in storage. She lost it somehow in the recent transfer of clothes to Wendy's store in the alleyway. Then one of the many crows—which visit the fruit trees on the other side of the same alley—picked up the sparkly item and stowed it away in his nest."

She grinned at Mack. "A quarry of sorts in the quince."

Chapter 25

DOREEN AND MACK walked slowly down the river. "You should be thankful I brought you in on the action, before the gunmen even arrived," she complained good-naturedly. For the last twenty minutes he'd been lecturing her steadily about staying out of trouble.

He sighed. "You know that I am really happy about that, as it shows you're learning."

"I *am* learning," she confirmed. "I still think I should learn how to handle a gun though."

He reached up a hand, crossed his heart, and said, "Please not."

"Why not?" she cried out. "I think it would be a good idea."

"Of course you would, but I'm not sure my heart can handle it."

She chuckled. "I think your heart's doing just fine."

"Maybe," he muttered, "but you are one scary person. How did you figure all that out?"

"I don't know. Just some of those pieces came together, while I figured out the rest." As they walked closer to Nan's, she added, "I'm glad it's over."

"You and me both." And then he laughed. "And now you definitely have enough money to get through the next few months."

She turned and beamed at him. "Isn't that awesome? Bernard gave me a check right then and there for the ten thousand dollar reward." And then she stopped. "But it's a check." She looked at Mack, worried. "What if it doesn't clear the bank?"

Mack smiled. "I'm pretty sure you know where he lives, so, if the check bounces, I'm certain you can go get another one."

She sighed. "He wouldn't do that, would he?"

"No, I don't think he would. I'm pretty sure that the richest developer in the city is good for that kind of money."

"But he already got insurance money for the theft of it."

"Yep, which I presume he will repay. Again, that won't stop your little check from clearing the bank. Just think of this from Bernard's point of view. He got so much more than his diamond ring back. Finding that ring and returning it to its rightful owner has now put *paid* to that stage of his life, where he feels like he got ripped off."

"And look at that," she added. "You guys may almost be friends outta this."

He shrugged. "He seems like kind of a nice guy."

"In spite of himself, right?"

He laughed. "I'm not that hard to please," he stated, "as long as I know he's not after you."

She looped her arm through his. "Even if he was, it wouldn't make a darn bit of difference. Apparently I'm an idiot, and I happen to like big lugheads, like you."

He burst out laughing, squeezed her arm, and nodded. "I don't know about the insults, but I'm okay as long as they're said in that sexy tone of voice."

"Exactly," she murmured. "Besides, you know I only mean it in good fun."

At that, he laughed. "That's what they all say," he teased. "Have you told Nan about the reward money?"

"I haven't really had a chance. I figured we'd do that tonight, when we go see her."

"Sounds good to me. I presume that's where we're heading."

"Yep, a cup of tea at Nan's. That's what the animals need too." She watched them gallivanting around happily. "Thaddeus wants to go back and visit with his new friends soon at the quince tree too."

"Is that where he learned that trick to capture shiny objects, do you think?"

"I don't know where else. It's the only place that we have recently been around birds," she admitted, smiling.

"It is pretty amazing though, when you think about it."

"What?"

"How well you figured that out," he admitted. "I never have enough time to spend on things like that."

"And I keep telling you that it's really not about the time. It's all about the people involved and how much time has gone by since everything blew up."

"I wonder," he muttered.

"I mean, once you give it time—so that many things can shake loose—that's why cold cases have to be revisited every once in a while," she noted. "Just to make it all happen."

"Maybe," he muttered. "I have told everybody at the office."

"I'm sure you have." She chuckled. "What did they say?"

"Everything from *I should marry you* to *watch my back*."

While laughing, he looked at her sideways.

"Yeah, speaking of marriage," she added, "your brother left me a voice mail on my phone to call him."

"Good, maybe it's something final this time regarding your divorce."

"Even if it's progress, I'd be happy with that."

"Me too," he muttered. "When will you call him?"

"Maybe tomorrow. Tonight's a whole different story. We'll go spend some time with Nan. That's family that I understand," she explained. "Some of this other stuff is just a little too … too beyond me."

He laughed. "Now *that* I don't believe. Nothing's too beyond you." He leaned over, gave her a kiss on her temple, and said, "You're pretty amazing. You know that, right?"

She looked up at him and beamed. "So are you."

"And why is that?" he asked.

"You're getting very well trained," she teased, with an innocent look on her face.

He frowned. "I don't think I like where this is going."

"Nonsense. I called, and you came running. Now that's perfect. *Perfectly trained.*"

He groaned. "I'll never live that one down, will I?"

She burst out laughing. "You will one day. But not for a while yet."

And, with that, they headed down the river to Nan's.

Epilogue

Tuesday Evening

A FEW DAYS later she was repeating the same pattern, walking down to Nan's with Mack. "This is becoming a bit of a habit."

"Is two times a habit?" he asked.

"Maybe."

"Well, this time I have to be there because Nan is hosting a celebration for you."

She chuckled. "I told her not to bother."

"Yep, but you also know how much she loves doing this kind of stuff."

"Yeah, that's true," she murmured. "She really does have fun, doesn't she?"

"And so she should. It's important to her."

Doreen nodded. "And anything that's important to Nan is important to me."

"Although I'm not too sure that I want Bernard there though," Mack noted in an odd tone.

"You're fine to have Bernard there," she replied immediately, "because he doesn't matter to me, not in that way."

"Well, at least my brother has got your ex working on

some paperwork now to get this divorce of yours settled."

"I know. Isn't that huge?" She clapped her hands. "Also I have a message from Scott at the auction house, but I couldn't reach him directly. Something about the antiques. He said it was good news though."

"Yay," Mack said. "You got the ten grand reward from Bernard, and of course you shared it with Esther, and, with any luck, Nick is making progress on your divorce, plus money from the antiques auction might be coming too? And you'll be in the money before you know it."

"I'm feeling pretty cheeky about money right now," she admitted. "I know ten thousand isn't much. But, as I said, until you have to sell your clothing to buy food to eat, you don't know what shame and poor is."

"But I liked your response," he replied quietly. "It shows your priorities are right."

"I hope so," she murmured. "How will Candy be in all this?"

"Better than I think she expects. I mean, she had physical possession of the real diamond for ten years, yet she didn't know it wasn't the fake ring. Although she technically didn't do anything illegal, she was still part of the original chaos about stealing one expensive diamond ring," he added, "so that will be the only issue. I've left it with the DA to sort out, but I suspect she will get off with some fairly small sentence or probation, if anything at all. She was there, helping to solve it at the end. At least that's how she put it. Something about the way you suggested that she say it."

Doreen shrugged. "Well, she didn't complain when I called for the police to give us a hand," she noted, still beaming. "So, as far as I'm concerned, she helped solve it at the end, and she should be let off the hook. Besides, she has been going to therapy for a long time, will continue going, and seems intent on rehabilitating herself."

"I know," Mack admitted. "And anything that she can do to get herself back on track is huge."

Doreen nodded. "I agree. It's pretty sad when we see the same people committing crimes time and time again."

Mack nodded.

As they came around the corner of the greenway, heading toward Nan's, Doreen looked up at the sky and sighed. "It's a perfect evening for this."

"And everybody'll be there," he said, chuckling.

"Well, I could do without that," she groaned.

They came up to the huge rosebush alongside the pathway, leading from the parking lot to the front door of Rosemoor.

She smiled and said, "Aren't they beautiful?"

"I didn't think they bloomed at this time of year."

She nodded. "Roses can bloom for a very long time, if they're well tended to. Kind of like revenge."

He looked at her in surprise. "Where did that come from?" he asked.

She shrugged, gave him a little smirk. "You know, like, *Revenge in the Roses*."

He rolled his eyes. "How about you just take a break from all these cases?"

"Maybe," she said cheerfully. "I intend to enjoy tonight at least."

"Good."

They walked the last few steps, and a man stepped out from a vehicle, called out to Mack, "Hey, copper."

Mack turned toward him and frowned. "What's the matter? Can I help you?"

"Absolutely you can. You can die." And, with that, he shot Mack. He fired a second shot at Doreen, but she had already dropped beside Mack, who'd fallen into the rosebush. He called out, "Revenge is best served cold." And, with a hard laugh, he added, "And now you're dead too." And he bolted away in a vehicle, tearing off as fast as it could go.

All Doreen could do—as she tried to stop the bleeding in Mack's upper chest—was think about her words. *Revenge in the Roses.* Had she helped make this happen?

This concludes Book 17 of Lovely Lethal Gardens: Quarry in the Quince.

Read about Revenge in the Roses: Lovely Lethal Gardens, Book 18

Lovely Lethal Gardens: Revenge in the Roses (Book #18)

A new cozy mystery series from *USA Today* best-selling author Dale Mayer. Follow gardener and amateur sleuth Doreen Montgomery—and her amusing and mostly lovable cat, dog, and parrot—as they catch murderers and solve crimes in lovely Kelowna, British Columbia.

Riches to rags. ... Bullets start flying. ... Rage is rising, ... especially for some!

When the journey to Rosemoor for a celebratory evening turns deadly, Doreen's life is flipped on her head. She can only watch in horror as Mack is shot right in front of her. Horrified, she vows to solve this case and fast, before the shooter realizes he failed and comes back for a second attempt.

Corporal Mack Moreau has been shot before, but this

time it's way worse because Doreen watched it all happen. Now she's planning to catch the shooter before Mack even starts to heal. That's not a good idea. She's yet to consider that maybe the shooter wasn't after Mack but really wanted to shoot her. After all, the cases she's been involved in have created a whole new level of acquaintances in her life. How many of them are gunning for her?

But Doreen is not deterred, and, with her trusty team at her side, she's determined to keep Mack safe by finding his shooter before he tries again.

Find Book 18 here!

To find out more visit Dale Mayer's website.

https://smarturl.it/DMSRevenge

Get Your Free Book Now!

Have you met Charmin Marvin?

If you're ready for a new world to explore, and love ill-mannered cats, I have a series that might be your next binge read. It's called Broken Protocols, and it's a series that takes you through time-travel, mysteries, romance… and a talking cat named Charmin Marvin.

Go here and tell me where to send it!
http://smarturl.it/ArsenicBofB

Author's Note

Thank you for reading Quarry in the Quince: Lovely Lethal Gardens, Book 17! If you enjoyed the book, please take a moment and leave a short review.

Dear reader,

I love to hear from readers, and you can contact me at my website: www.dalemayer.com or at my Facebook author page. To be informed of new releases and special offers, sign up for my newsletter or follow me on BookBub. And if you are interested in joining Dale Mayer's Reader Group, here is the Facebook sign up page.
https://smarturl.it/DaleMayerFBGroup

Cheers,
Dale Mayer

About the Author

Dale Mayer is a *USA Today* best-selling author, best known for her SEALs military romances, her Psychic Visions series, and her Lovely Lethal Garden cozy series. Her contemporary romances are raw and full of passion and emotion (Broken But ... Mending, Hathaway House series). Her thrillers will keep you guessing (Kate Morgan, By Death series), and her romantic comedies will keep you giggling (*It's a Dog's Life*, a stand-alone novella; and the Broken Protocols series, starring Charming Marvin, the cat).

Dale honors the stories that come to her—and some of them are crazy, break all the rules and cross multiple genres!

To go with her fiction, she also writes nonfiction in many different fields, with books available on résumé writing, companion gardening, and the US mortgage system. All her books are available in print and ebook format.

Connect with Dale Mayer Online

Dale's Website – www.dalemayer.com
Twitter – @DaleMayer
Facebook – facebook.com/DaleMayer.author
BookBub – bookbub.com/authors/dale-mayer

Also by Dale Mayer

Published Adult Books:

Shadow Recon
Magnus, Book 1

Bullard's Battle
Ryland's Reach, Book 1
Cain's Cross, Book 2
Eton's Escape, Book 3
Garret's Gambit, Book 4
Kano's Keep, Book 5
Fallon's Flaw, Book 6
Quinn's Quest, Book 7
Bullard's Beauty, Book 8
Bullard's Best, Book 9
Bullard's Battle, Books 1–2
Bullard's Battle, Books 3–4
Bullard's Battle, Books 5–6
Bullard's Battle, Books 7–8

Terkel's Team
Damon's Deal, Book 1
Wade's War, Book 2
Gage's Goal, Book 3
Calum's Contact, Book 4

Kate Morgan

Simon Says... Hide, Book 1
Simon Says... Jump, Book 2
Simon Says... Ride, Book 3
Simon Says... Scream, Book 4
Simon Says... Run, Book 5

Hathaway House

Aaron, Book 1
Brock, Book 2
Cole, Book 3
Denton, Book 4
Elliot, Book 5
Finn, Book 6
Gregory, Book 7
Heath, Book 8
Iain, Book 9
Jaden, Book 10
Keith, Book 11
Lance, Book 12
Melissa, Book 13
Nash, Book 14
Owen, Book 15
Percy, Book 16
Quinton, Book 17
Hathaway House, Books 1–3
Hathaway House, Books 4–6
Hathaway House, Books 7–9

The K9 Files

Ethan, Book 1
Pierce, Book 2

Zane, Book 3
Blaze, Book 4
Lucas, Book 5
Parker, Book 6
Carter, Book 7
Weston, Book 8
Greyson, Book 9
Rowan, Book 10
Caleb, Book 11
Kurt, Book 12
Tucker, Book 13
Harley, Book 14
Kyron, Book 15
Jenner, Book 16
The K9 Files, Books 1–2
The K9 Files, Books 3–4
The K9 Files, Books 5–6
The K9 Files, Books 7–8
The K9 Files, Books 9–10
The K9 Files, Books 11–12

Lovely Lethal Gardens
Arsenic in the Azaleas, Book 1
Bones in the Begonias, Book 2
Corpse in the Carnations, Book 3
Daggers in the Dahlias, Book 4
Evidence in the Echinacea, Book 5
Footprints in the Ferns, Book 6
Gun in the Gardenias, Book 7
Handcuffs in the Heather, Book 8
Ice Pick in the Ivy, Book 9
Jewels in the Juniper, Book 10

Killer in the Kiwis, Book 11
Lifeless in the Lilies, Book 12
Murder in the Marigolds, Book 13
Nabbed in the Nasturtiums, Book 14
Offed in the Orchids, Book 15
Poison in the Pansies, Book 16
Quarry in the Quince, Book 17
Revenge in the Roses, Book 18
Lovely Lethal Gardens, Books 1–2
Lovely Lethal Gardens, Books 3–4
Lovely Lethal Gardens, Books 5–6
Lovely Lethal Gardens, Books 7–8
Lovely Lethal Gardens, Books 9–10

Psychic Vision Series
Tuesday's Child
Hide 'n Go Seek
Maddy's Floor
Garden of Sorrow
Knock Knock…
Rare Find
Eyes to the Soul
Now You See Her
Shattered
Into the Abyss
Seeds of Malice
Eye of the Falcon
Itsy-Bitsy Spider
Unmasked
Deep Beneath
From the Ashes
Stroke of Death

Ice Maiden
Snap, Crackle…
What If…
Talking Bones
Psychic Visions Books 1–3
Psychic Visions Books 4–6
Psychic Visions Books 7–9

By Death Series
Touched by Death
Haunted by Death
Chilled by Death
By Death Books 1–3

Broken Protocols – Romantic Comedy Series
Cat's Meow
Cat's Pajamas
Cat's Cradle
Cat's Claus
Broken Protocols 1-4

Broken and… Mending
Skin
Scars
Scales (of Justice)
Broken but… Mending 1-3

Glory
Genesis
Tori
Celeste
Glory Trilogy

Biker Blues

Morgan: Biker Blues, Volume 1

Cash: Biker Blues, Volume 2

SEALs of Honor

Mason: SEALs of Honor, Book 1

Hawk: SEALs of Honor, Book 2

Dane: SEALs of Honor, Book 3

Swede: SEALs of Honor, Book 4

Shadow: SEALs of Honor, Book 5

Cooper: SEALs of Honor, Book 6

Markus: SEALs of Honor, Book 7

Evan: SEALs of Honor, Book 8

Mason's Wish: SEALs of Honor, Book 9

Chase: SEALs of Honor, Book 10

Brett: SEALs of Honor, Book 11

Devlin: SEALs of Honor, Book 12

Easton: SEALs of Honor, Book 13

Ryder: SEALs of Honor, Book 14

Macklin: SEALs of Honor, Book 15

Corey: SEALs of Honor, Book 16

Warrick: SEALs of Honor, Book 17

Tanner: SEALs of Honor, Book 18

Jackson: SEALs of Honor, Book 19

Kanen: SEALs of Honor, Book 20

Nelson: SEALs of Honor, Book 21

Taylor: SEALs of Honor, Book 22

Colton: SEALs of Honor, Book 23

Troy: SEALs of Honor, Book 24

Axel: SEALs of Honor, Book 25

Baylor: SEALs of Honor, Book 26

Hudson: SEALs of Honor, Book 27

Heroes for Hire

SEALs of Steel

The Mavericks

Collections

Standalone Novellas

Published Young Adult Books:

Family Blood Ties Series
Vampire in Denial
Vampire in Distress
Vampire in Design
Vampire in Deceit
Vampire in Defiance
Vampire in Conflict
Vampire in Chaos
Vampire in Crisis
Vampire in Control
Vampire in Charge
Family Blood Ties Set 1–3
Family Blood Ties Set 1–5
Family Blood Ties Set 4–6
Family Blood Ties Set 7–9
Sian's Solution, A Family Blood Ties Series Prequel
    Novelette

Design series
Dangerous Designs
Deadly Designs
Darkest Designs
Design Series Trilogy

Standalone
In Cassie's Corner
Gem Stone (a Gemma Stone Mystery)
Time Thieves

Published Non-Fiction Books:

Career Essentials

Career Essentials: The Résumé

Career Essentials: The Cover Letter

Career Essentials: The Interview

Career Essentials: 3 in 1